NARICAN
THE
CLOAKED
DECEPTION

This book is a work of fiction. The names, characters, places, and incidents are products of the writer's imagination or have been used fictitiously and are not to be construed as real. Any resemblance to persons—living or dead—actual events, locales, or organizations is entirely coincidental.

Narican: The Cloaked Deception
Published by Douglas Robbins
Cover Design by Damonza.com
Edited by Athans Associates
Copyright © 2019 by Douglas Robbins
ISBN: 978-1-7333978-0-3
www.dmrobbinsauthor.com

Hold close what is most precious, or your ene-
mies will gladly strip it away.

—Narican Prophet Muzzana

THE RECKONING HAS BEGUN

Up close, a thin man kneels. His forehead pulsates a soft blue light like a flickering nightlight from under the cowl of a black robe that covers much of his elongated face. His lips do not move yet words come forth.

"Ancestor of the great beyond, hear me. I seek your wisdom."

A gray cloaked shimmering man with three eyes appears upon a mountaintop of black onyx. His third eye resides in the lower portion of his forehead, forming a triangle with the lower two. Around the third eye's edges, flecks sparkle as if heated coal embers. Emerald colored complex math equations hover in the air alongside him.

"What troubles you, Tanz, Son of Requiten?" His emerald green third eye sparkles while two black eyes remain fixed below.

"Toxic Whisperers sweep through the dimensions like a storm. Narican has fallen under their rule. It is the seat of the highest sentient beings."

"Yes, and the home you were cast from. Unsettling, yet this is not the sole reason of your troubles."

The kneeling man shakes his head while his forehead pulsates blue. "We were blind to this attack and did not see. These perpetrators hid themselves from the universal records. Yet I do not understand how." Clearly vexed, the kneeling man continues, "My equation and the records must be incomplete. I have failed you and Narican."

The specter closes his black eyes, searching for answers, while his radiant emerald eye remains open, dilating. "Your equation is infallible. Crevasses within the universe, even light beings cannot see."

"In the past they were unable to perpetrate this. How did they come to circumnavigate universal knowledge?" His forehead pulsates where a third eye would be if standing upon Narican, his home.

"They have learned, Tanz. Evolved in their wickedness. The dark forces of the Toxic Whisperers always seek to exploit and corrupt."

"These criminals are hidden, and now here, infiltrating this planet."

The ancestor appears perplexed by this information. "In the third dimension?"

"Yes. I have witnessed the scouts, the haze clusters."

"Hmm, this has eluded my sight. They may be clouding the energy channels. A powerful being is behind this."

"But who? What do they want? Why now?"

"That, you must find out. If darkness reigns, the higher and lower dimensions will be lost. The gods of light will grow blind and disconnected like a flower pulled from its roots."

"This is why I seek your council."

"We can guide, yet cannot intervene with the living. Laws even we cannot defy. Enough blood has been lost, no?"

The man's forehead pulsates blue. "By my accounting, more must be. These humans are vulnerable, weak sentient beings and easy prey for the dark forces."

"I see your concerns. The human mind and spirit are often at war, misaligned with their higher purpose. Yet several do strive for alignment with their souls' abilities, whereas many remain, never to advance."

"It is only a theory," the kneeling man projects, "yet they may attempt to prevent this alignment by submerging humans into permanent darkness."

"And this will break the evolving chain of souls...Troubling indeed."

"Thank you for speaking with me, Ancestor. Though there is one last thing. The boy, King Oneon's son, is now of age. He does not know of my existence and does not know himself or our history. He too struggles with the Dichotomy, the torn mind."

"At the right moment he will know you. He cannot do this alone, nor can you. To find answers he will need you and you will need him. These are dangerous times indeed for the living. Sentient beings are at stake. This is not the order of things. If unsuccessful, souls will be severed from their higher purposes, from the gods, and cast into eternal darkness.

"But be forewarned, Tanz, the humans are cunning and destructive of what they do not understand. Reveal only what is necessary. As the dark forces will also know the boy's age, you must watch him closely."

"When shall I act? His surrogate family was terminated after another attempt on his life."

The specter closes his black eyes again while his green one remains open. "Impulse will call upon you. Listen to her. The intelligence of the universe will guide you to action."

Blue pulsations cease, and the man now kneels alone inside a messy apartment with white walls, a tattered blue couch, and clothes strewn about. Opening his blue, intelligent eyes he rises and walks to a window. Opening the blinds, he peers out upon a busy city.

THE HAUNTED BOY

"Run, Claremone!" I hear over the clamor rising from the surprise attack. A spreading dark haze blows into the room. Familiar voices call to me. I am running. Perhaps five or six years old. My feet sluggish. We are running in terror inside the royal onyx palace as the heat of battle swells. Guards lower their lancers with illuminated spears standing at the ready to defend, but they are swiftly swallowed by the growing haze enclosing around them. Gone like ash in the wind.

Cornered by this nameless, faceless evil. One by one I see everyone about to die. Dark blades of mist coming down to take us all.

My mind snaps awake, and eyes strain left and right, scanning my little apartment, making certain I am alone. Dream energy fills the space.

My small desk, chair, end table, and throw rug by the door are as they were last night. It's summertime in Big City. My pillow is soaked with sweat. This haunting dream has become nightly and clearer whereas just a few weeks ago it was vague and distant, scattered throughout my childhood.

Kicking off the top sheet and thin blanket, I place feet on the floor rubbing my face and red stubble. A rusty sun comes through the blinds. I wonder again as I have for the past week, if I died in this other world. Reading once that if we die in dreams we die in life.

Arguments rise from the city streets below. Something big is going to happen, I just don't know what. The cauldron of humanity is already spilling over with anger and arguments everywhere I go. Each era has its own catastrophe: tsunamis, earthquakes, stock market crashes, war, disease.

The history books say one is coming for us. Sunlight radiates through my two windows, yet even the sun doesn't look right lately, more rust colored than yellow.

Shaking off these dark thoughts I reach for the *Tao Te Ching* on my nightstand and feel my breathing slow. Opening the book, I allow the words to soothe my conflicted mind. Allowing it to open and land where it will…

Mastering others is strength; mastering yourself is true power.

I nod, staring at building tops out the window knowing hundreds of people fill each building story with their own individual stories.

I flip a few more pages.

A man with outward courage dares to die; a man with inner courage dares to live.

I've read this one before and thought about it many times. People, I've noticed, myself included, are more often afraid of living than of dying.

And lastly…

Give evil nothing to oppose and it will disappear by itself.

I bounce off the bed. Sometimes a little is all I need.

My thick wavy red hair and green eyes reflect in the window. Like the yin and yang, my birthname is Reuben yet in dreams it's Claremone. I know that doesn't make sense. Nothing makes much sense. The question—Who am I?—tears at me. I need answers, not dreams, not voices, but answers.

Let me start with the little I know. A few months back, my parents, Robert and Jan, were killed in a car accident.

We were driving home after a hike at Blue Falls State Park, it was daytime, and no animal jumped in front of us. It wasn't even raining, but the car skidded off the road and hit a tree, killing them instantly.

I remember seeing the steering wheel turn as if on its own. My father fought it. "I can't stop it… Jan. Jan. Jan!" he shouted, glancing my mother's way. His round, intelligent eyes filled with worry while my mother's small hands dug into the dashboard.

"Robert, no. Not this way!" she said in a meek, panicked voice.

From the dense forest, shadows closed in around the car. Powerless, I sat in the rear like an idiot, doing nothing. Could I have helped? Maybe.

Parts of the memory don't make sense though I've run through it a hundred times. Hands were on me then I woke at the hospital. My psychiatrist,

Dr. Greenblatt, said those were the hands of the paramedics. But they couldn't be. Something protected me when that tree hit that car, someone or something. If not, I would have been crushed, too.

I wipe my nose, grabbing my parent's picture from the nightstand. We'd had a picnic in the backyard the day the picture was taken. Our Black Lab, Rufus, ate half the hot dogs off the table.

Chills tickle my body and I set their picture down. My hands grow cold. Though high summer, I pull the covers over my legs.

Skyscrapers poke cloud's bellies above cabs, noise, and decay. All the kooks and crazies are down there, maybe some answers, too.

There's a burning in me to find answers and learn what happened. With cells on fire, I sure wasn't going to find them in our suburban development where all houses and lawns look alike.

Today I turned eighteen, yay, and know there's something I can't quite put my finger on about this world. The questions burn in my chest, linger behind my eyes and thoughts, something deep, buried, far away. Like a memory I can't quite recall.

So now I live in the craziest place in the world, where my red hair and green eyes go unnoticed. With so many weird styles, hair colors, tribal tattoos, and piercings, people just doing their thing, living some meaning they've found for themselves.

I try to be a good person. My parents taught me that.

I work at a small food market a few blocks over on Vexington, though today's my day off.

So, pizza day and a stop at Caesar's, my one friend in town.

I head outside with blue jeans, black t-shirt, and a ball cap. After all, I do have sensitive skin and burn easily.

*

With a hot sun overhead, hungry for pizza yet even hungrier for answers, I stop at Other Worlds three blocks over—the mystical shop where Caesar works. That's where we met. The bells bounce and chime as the door latches behind me.

"The dream's getting worse..." I say, leaning against it.

"Well, come in, let's pull some cards on you."

This is a safe space for seekers. And Caesar, being a seeker himself, is never worried about taboo subjects, or needing to be some stereotypical guy.

The lights are dim with smiling buddhas and crystals on store shelves with bookcases lining the wall. A waterfall trickles.

The incense burns my nose like chemicals as I walk up. Standing behind the glass counter a few inches taller than me he sports a black goatee with black hair and dark skin. "I'm gonna go crazy soon or take those pills Dr. G. gave me."

"You're not taking those nasty pills that hack prescribed."

He goes into a spokesman-like voice. "They help with delusional tendencies, yet side effects may include loss of bladder control, stinky armpits, madness, uncontrollable rage, rashes, flatulence, and death. Order now!" He returns to his regular Big City accent. "Sounds great, chief. Sign me up. The answer is always inside of us."

"I don't know, but it's getting worse. Can't tell what's real anymore."

"Well, I'm real…" He pokes me in the chest. "Ya see? Dreams can't poke you."

He bends. "Let me get a special deck Nan Nan keeps down here." Nan Nan is his grandmother he runs the store with.

"Thanks."

"Nan Nan uses these for troubled souls such as yourself." He spreads out the old Tarot deck with images of animals, dragons, kings, and treasures. Many cards are curled at their corners.

"Pick three."

I choose slowly, overlooking the deck. A few protrude out, almost hitting me in the belly. I pull three and hold them up so he can't see.

"Uh, I'm not a mind reader, dude. This isn't poker. You have to lay them down."

I nod placing them on top of the spread cards.

"An upside-down king, a flaming Phoenix, and dueling Dragons."

"Well, what do they mean?"

"How should I know?" He grabs a book and flips to a chart that coincides with the numbers on the lower left hand of each card then flips to the right page for the upside-down king.

Caesar reads, " 'The cards will come to you as either an ally or challenger.

When upside down, it's a challenger. This one says events are turning your life upside down; you may be feeling dizzy and confused. You may feel like life is unfair right now. Do whatever is necessary to bring your life back into balance. You will be grateful when balance is restored and the rollercoaster has ended.' "

I admit that feels close to home. I pick up the next card, the flaming red Phoenix and ask him to read it.

Flipping pages, Caesar reads, " 'The Phoenix appears as your ally to celebrate your journey and ensure your ultimate success. This is true even if it appears you've just passed through a metaphorical experience or death, or are currently enduring a perception of failure in your life. Death and rebirth are related in the realm of the Phoenix. Whatever you do now, a rebirth is imminent.' "

I'm reminded of the recent death of my parents and feel a stabbing pain in my chest. Some rebirth, being all alone.

"What about this last card? It says the Dragon's Duel."

"Hmmmm… Let me see." Caesar finds the page and reads, " 'The Dueling Dragons take place at the proverbial fork in the road. It is both ally and challenger, representing the tension of opposites. Even though the truth is that we live in unity, we experience the duality of faith and doubt, right and wrong, love and fear. If you're torn between two dragons, the one you choose to feed will be the one that wins.' "

"So, what does all this mean?"

He closes his eyes and is silent for a moment before murmuring, "That you will bring me a slice of pizza from Sal's." His eyes pop open. "I don't know, man. Nan Nan's not here." She's usually at church on Sundays with rosary beads, kneeling in prayer.

His eyes close again. "A storm is coming." His voice deepens and he places his hands on the cards. "The gift of seeing is without eyes. People walk around and don't see nothin'."

I glance out the window. "It's sunny and warm." I shrug. "Maybe some rain." I look back at him.

"See with your essence, not your mind." Caesar slams his hand down on the counter. "Listen!" he says, raising his voice. "A storm is coming to claim you. You must not let it. Others see us as we are. I. See. You." He then stops, opening his eyes again. "You're still here. Going to Sal's or what? You know I can't leave."

"Come on, are you messing with me?"

"What do you mean? Are you buying incense or need a book?" he asks, shaking his head.

"No, I'm good. But do I owe you anything for the reading?"

He stares down at the Tarot cards. "Wow, I totally forgot we did that. Hmm. Nah, all good."

We move to the exit and the bright, noisy day. With the door now open I look at the busyness of the city as heat and humidity attach to my shirt.

"In that dream I keep dying. Do you think we've lived, or, I guess, died before?"

He places his hand on my shoulder. "Nan Nan says we leave pieces of ourselves places and can only return to them when we're ready."

I nod, pondering this, not entirely sure what it means.

"Thanks, C. I always feel better coming here. I never had a brother, you know?"

"And I never had a sister," he says, slapping my back.

I laugh, letting go of the door. I step onto the sidewalk to reenter the deep waters of Big City. Confused by this new information, I slip into the flow of pedestrians heading in the direction of Sal's.

An upside down king... the Phoenix... and what did he say about the Dueling Dragons? My thoughts bulge with noise and information crashing into one another.

But do I really believe in some silly cards?

My head is splitting in two. I try my breathing exercises, breathing deep, feeling my feet on the pavement, feel my breath connecting with my higher self. Who am I? Who am I? Who am I?

My belly tightens as my taste buds salivate. Thoughts of hunger drag me away. Oh man, one block from Sal's and I can smell the garlic and homemade sauce. But what did Caesar mean that a storm was coming? I look up, one black cloud does hang low in a blue sky.

Some slick looking guy in a blue suit and black sunglasses stands next to me at the street corner. He smells of money, sizing me up with a scowl like

I'm not in his league and don't belong here. We're crammed together waiting for the light to change. The walk sign illuminates and a mass of bodies move.

I wonder why he keeps glancing at me. Screw him. I have every right to walk here. It's a free country, mostly.

He sways his head to music. I look away, but when I look back, he's panicked. Smoke rises from his hand as the music player bursts into flames. Melting plastic, warbling sounds… he tries throwing it, but can't let go. It seems glued to his skin, burning his hand.

After several attempts it drops to the ground, the plastic smashing apart. He stomps on the dead device, clutching his burned hand. I can almost feel the pain shoot up my arm.

A group gathers. The businessman bends getting his face closer to the charred remains. He glances up at me then yells at the player. "I won't do it! He's too weak looking. No. I said, No!" he shouts again then takes off at a sprint, disappearing around the next street corner.

I can feel anger and confusion everywhere. I know the unseen world is trying to break through. Everything feels on edge.

I turn back down the sidewalk and a thud hits me in the chest—hands knocking me back. Outside a tattoo parlor this giant man with crazy brown curly hair, unshaved whiskers, and flaring nostrils has hatred in his eyes as if I murdered someone he loved.

He waves his hands. "Get the hell out of here! You're trouble for us," he says, striking me in the chest again. I stumble toward the curb. He charges me, punching me in the stomach. Air leaves my body. Throat tightens, can't breathe, eyes water, vision clouds.

People point and laugh. "Check out the big guy. He's going to kill that dude. Let's see what happens. Sal's can wait." Voices speak from around my age.

I look for a cop or someone to save me, but there's no one. My parents are gone. I'm alone in this cold world. Something isn't right. No one has ever come at me before. I'm scared and shaking.

"Look at that freak. He's so weird," a couple of other kids say. Older people point and laugh indifferently. "He must have it coming. They always do. Come, Linda, let's buy you that dress you want." An older man grabs a woman's arm. Advertisements play on storefront monitors.

What happened to them? There's no kindness. Who are these people? What happened to goodness?

Angry Burly Man pushes me again, knocking off my hat. His teeth show within a twisted grin, almost knocking me in front of a city bus. My head whiplashes, feeling the impact in my chest. He's too big. I can't fight him using the Tae Kwon Do I learned when I was fourteen.

I plead with him, "Sir, I'm no one. I'm no one. I'm sorry, whatever I did."

He hovers so close I can smell his B.O. "Go away and don't come back. Next time I won't be so nice. Your time is over here, boy. You and your kind." He laughs. Others join him.

"But I'm just a store clerk."

"Don't lie to me." He tightens a fist to punch: a hand so large it would cave in my face. He then releases his fist and slaps himself in the face. "I hate lies…" he says through grinding teeth, pauses, then stomps back to the shop, slamming the door.

"Me too," I say to his back, out of breath.

The store lights flip off. Standing in the darkness with arms crossed his eyes dart up and down the block. He then stares at me through the storefront window and chills run through me.

My time is over here? My kind? What does that mean? I don't have a "kind."

Embarrassed and ashamed, people stare at me. I need to ask him what he means, but don't dare. He seems to know something about me. I, me, Reuben, an eighteen year old grocery store clerk. A threat to no one other than myself. A no one. The same chills trickle over me I felt this morning looking at my parents' picture, remembering the accident.

The black cloud overhead has lifted, and now feel the hot sun burning my scalp.

My head spins and my chest hurts. I'm nauseous and hungry. Is Claremone a dream? Dr. G and my parents always said, "No, No, No. He's not real."

In the dark store Angry Burly Man, a stranger, stares out at me.

I turn slightly to elude his glare when a woman's voice echoes off the buildings,

"They are coming for you, child. They are coming."

I spin around, looking for her. A voice I'd only heard in dreams. Nothing but city in all directions. Ravenous, I turn for home and run, forgetting about the slices, feeling like a vulnerable animal out in the open.

UNSETTLED AND ALONE

AFTER CLOSING THE door to my fifth-floor walkup apartment, my arm hairs bristle sensing someone's in here. I check for Angry Burly Man inside the closet behind winter coats, long sleeve shirts, behind the shower curtain and bathroom door, though he'd need to be paper thin to fit back there. I check anyway. Under my bed, in the fridge, I don't find anyone.

In the bathroom mirror I lift my shirt, flinching at the fist size bruises. Movement catches the corner of my eye, I step quickly into the living room which is also my bedroom. There's no one here, yet I have this eerie sense a crowd watches me from afar, waiting. They shimmer briefly like kicked up dust then disappear. Must've been sunlight reflecting off particles. The maid hasn't come this month to clean.

I should definitely call Dr. Greenblatt. He'd prescribe that awful medicine again, Proxylipitan. To help with my overactive imagination and mood disorders, dumb me down. I didn't like the way it made me feel, like a stupor after not sleeping for a night.

Calming, feeling safer now, hunger takes over. Scrounging around the cupboard I grab a jar of all-natural creamy peanut butter, expired one month ago. A big perk of the job is taking home expired food. Yum. I lean against the counter eating it by the spoonful.

My mother told me people with anger issues are only scared and injured somewhere deep inside. Was Angry Burly Man scared of me? He sure didn't seem scared when he hit me.

Maybe a storm is coming, or maybe I'm just having a bad day. Maybe everyone is.

There must be a clue to my past. Something to point me in the right direction. I'm not crazy.

Over at my desk I put the peanut butter down and start looking closer at family pictures, seashells, ticket stubs, pulling out my desk drawer. There may be clues I never noticed. Links. Connections.

I look closer, remembering our tan house and driving into the Woodland Hills Community about forty miles from here, where each house rested on less than a quarter acre, with matching two car garage and well-trimmed hedges. It was hard to tell them apart except for the mailbox numbers and different colors.

I was ten when my mother and I walked in the development. A large brown sedan careened out of control. Diving into the bushes, we got cut up as the car skidded to a screeching halt up on the curb. The street sign clanged to the ground a foot in front of us. The driver was a gray-haired elderly man with round head and hairy ears. Leaving the driver side door open, he hobbled over.

"Are you two all right? I pumped the brakes, but I… I don't know what happened…" He stared at the car with the two front wheels up on the curb and yellow street sign lying on the grass in front of us. The pointy metal tip only a foot from my face.

"I'm terribly sorry. I must be getting old, older." He rubbed his head in aged confusion as if events and memories were the same jumbled train running through his mind: less distinct, edges frayed, details murky.

"Sir, we're fine. Just a little shaken up," my mother said, brushing me off. "Are you, all right?" The bumper of his car had caved in where he hit the pole.

"I… I don't know," he responded absently.

She looked at me with accusation in her soft, small eyes. "That was a close call, sweetie. Too close this time." As if it was my fault.

We fell silent walking home. I glanced back at the man. In the house she made chicken soup then leaned against the counter sipping hers, staring off. There was confusion in her face, pain.

During this time, I thought all kids experienced the same "bad luck" or "happenings," as my mom called them.

"No, sweetie, they don't. But why do you?"

Dropping the spoon into the peanut butter jar, an idea strikes me. Wait, that's what happened to my parents. They lost control of the car, except there were shadows. Walking that day, we had our backs turned when we dived. There could have been shadows, or he might've just lost control. Oh, I don't know.

But that wasn't the only time. Over the years things would "fall." She tried making light of them and started affectionately calling me her "little black cat." A hot iron almost fell on me; the cord hooked on my shoe. Another time when I was three or four, the lawnmower got away from my father and rolled within a few feet of where I played then it shut off. Somehow, I'd always be one step out of reach. But not today.

Cold now, I grab a hoodie, realizing tears are running down my cheeks. Missing them and our home, that boring dull flavorless place, I'd give anything to go back there.

Over the years my parents wondered about me. They'd say I didn't look like them. "He's so odd," they'd say when they thought I was asleep.

But they loved me despite the issues. There was football and hot soup on cold days, and they made sure my hair was properly parted on my way to school.

As the years passed, they'd sit me on the couch and stare. I overheard them once wondering if I'd been switched at birth by the hospital. "A common mistake," my father said. I laid in bed wondering too.

When I was four or five the night terrors came. I'd sit up in bed screaming. As if being kidnapped or murdered, Robert and Jan would burst in. She'd rock me back and forth, comforting me as I sobbed. My body burned. Her frizzy brown hair tickled my nose. My lanky father with his receding hairline and narrow face would sit until I calmed. Then he'd drape both arms around us. I'd look up afraid for them both.

Late at night they'd slink back to their room, droopy eyed, needing rest for work the next morning. I'd stare at the closet seeing anguished, horned faces, strange and distorted with misshapen eyes, urging me to enter, hearing moaning sounds as if people in pain.

I'd close my eyes tightly, covering my head with a pillow, hearing my dream name hauntingly repeated over and over again, "Clar-e-mone… Clar-e-mone… Clar-e-mone…"

I'd wake the next morning with sun pouring through the windows and a feeling of protective love. The closet only contained sneakers, shirts, and books strewn about.

So much comes back to me now that they're gone, as if memories are more alive, clearer than when they happened.

I look at a picture of my mother when she was young and in college. I asked her once if she'd ever heard a voice from the sky, beyond the horizon. She looked at me quizzically and placed her hand on my forehead. "No, dear, I haven't."

"Oh, okay then. Just messing around."

At twelve they brought me to Dr. Greenblatt, having tired of these issues. "I just can't deal with it anymore, Jan," My father said in the kitchen while I sat at the top of the stairs. "It's just too difficult."

Dr. Greenblatt was portly, bald, and sat with a yellow legal pad in his downtown office. He asked a lot of questions and because he was an authority, I answered them.

I told him sometimes I felt like Zeus, but lightning never comes to my hands, like my power has been lost. He sat and nodded.

That's when they first gave me the pills. In the waiting room he and my mother spoke.

"He has some sort of psychosis, Mrs. Mitchell. Has he hit his head recently?"

"A psychosis, oh no, Doctor. No, he has not."

After the psychiatrist I was brought to the school counselor then a priest. I was forced to say Our Father Who Art in Heaven until he was convinced I'd said enough of them my soul was saved. I clearly worried him.

There's commotion on the street below. I get up and stare out the blinds watching people come and go from stores and restaurants. Cars honk. People shout at each other. One guy slams his hands on a car hood. There's anger in all directions and the television news is always violent, pitting people against each other. It plays on storefronts, buses, lampposts, everywhere I go. I try not to watch, but it sinks in.

Looking up and down the block I wonder, am I really the same as them?

Just some schlub working day to day. I'm angry, too, where there's hurt inside. Rage wells up about my parents and dreams. I don't realize it but I'm bending the metal of the chair.

To stop the anger, I look at the buildings knowing there's people struggling inside of them. My hands extend out as an energy within commands me to stop their division and for them to pursue their higher calling.

"This is not their purpose," I hear that woman's voice again.

Energy builds from my torso. My knees tremble from its power. My center, or *dantian* grows warm, expecting buildings to bend and streets to clear. In the reflection my eyes grow wide, fingertips pulsating with the energy of the sun, concentration increasing, yet nothing happens.

Quickly exhausted from the attempt, my arms and eyelids grow heavy. Sweat drips from my brow as I tear off my hoodie.

What an idiot. I have read too many books and must be crazy like my mother and psychiatrist suggested. "But sweet," she also added, kissing my forehead.

Memories merge and tumble from life to dreams and back again. I've seen enough of this day as I shut the blinds to sit upon my chair of metal and cotton, closing my eyes to dream of Narican, my home. Only in dreams have I ever felt free. So I'll dream. Crazy or not.

THE FRAYING REALM

HUNTED, I WAKE sweating in these mortal clothes, in this meager existence. Flipping on my lamp scanning the room. Shadows shift and bend. Sitting up, the clock reads 5:45 am. Hitting the alarm before it goes off, a sliver of sun rises over buildings along the far river.

Laying in sleepy, dream drenched thoughts, I force myself up, throw on clothes, brush teeth, eat toast with butter, and exit the apartment for my shift at the store.

Feet hitting the hard sidewalk, my stomach churns, inhaling some rotting fleshy stench coming up from a sewer grate. I turn into an alley and dry heave. My first full day being eighteen after my official birth time last night at 11:57. Now achy, sick. Great. I pop in a piece of spearmint gum and keep walking.

It's early, the city's still waking up. I like these times. Strolling down the street, breathing deeper, the sickness subsides.

On lampposts imbedded television screens play videos of war, bombs, violence, then sports for a minute then back to the bombs then commercials play new products for us to buy.

It's as if something is trying to get us riled up, in a bad mood, before the sun is even up. Or maybe that's all the news there is, but I doubt it.

There's too much pressure on people. Along the sidewalk car doors slam. A good-looking couple accuse each other of infidelity, though I've only ever seen them be kind.

From my street I turn south onto Vexington Avenue and the volume of commuters increases like a widening river, rushing past in skirts and suits. Cars sit and honk, hands angrily slam dashboards waiting for lights to change. One guy on his cell phone bumps into me and continues walking without apology. I almost say something but he's already halfway down the block. Breathe. Feet on sidewalk. Breathe. Let the river go around.

At the market I yank open the screen door to enter. The store sells the basics: cereals, canned goods, chips, mac n' cheese, milk, juice, with a small produce area in the rear. It has three aisles five shopping carts deep and mostly serves neighborhood folks.

I begin the day checking stocked items in the aisles to see what's running low, write out a list, go into the storeroom or take down from shelves above. I rotate the older items neatly to the front while placing new ones in the rear. I find the repetition relaxing: soup, beans, chili. It gives me time to think.

My overall responsibilities include stocking shelves, produce, and cashiering. Mopping up once a week. We rotate the responsibility, but I don't mind it. After stocking I handle milk deliveries, rolling out hand trucks with milks, creamers, butters, juices. I switch to cashiering late in the morning. Two registers sit up front. Blue countertops with worn wood that show in a few spots. Older women on a budget shop this time of day, making mornings quiet and easy.

A THREAD PULLED

RINGING ONE WOMAN up with a green pepper, eggs, and a pint of milk, another woman in a purple robe stumbles in, almost crashes through our screen door.

Out of breath, she shouts, "A robbery. A robbery." She points across the busy street leaning on the metal door handle. People move along indifferently, as if in a fog.

My coworker Caitlin and I peer out. A beefy bearded guy with a belly wearing a black and gray flannel shirt pulls at a woman's pocketbook. We hear her cries through the screen door.

"He does know it's August, right?" Caitlin says, looking at me with one raised eyebrow.

We hear her pleas: "Stop. Get off. Someone help me. Please, help me." She struggles to fend him off. Her head swiveling back and forth for chivalry, assistance, some good Samaritan to help. But just like me yesterday, no one's coming.

There are no cops in sight. Just hustle and bustle. Commuters gawk as they walk past but nobody makes a move to help. I shake my head.

The woman in the purple robe shouts at us, "That's my friend Claire. Please help. She just lost her husband Buddy six months ago. Now this. Oh, what happened to my wonderful city?"

As the man, eyes from Purple Robe, Caitlin, and Green Peppers descend on me.

This is not the first crime this neighborhood has seen. In fact, they've been on the rise lately. Like everything else. And I'll admit, at times I've been desensitized, turning a blind eye. Wanting to help, but what am I supposed to do? Tackle a guy twice my size? I've tried. It ends up with me getting a black eye and him getting away. We usually call the cops, who come too late.

This guy looks like an angry lumberjack after a tree fell on his foot. Eyebrows thick, face intense, yanking on that purse. He probably carries three hundred pounds of meanness and this little lady of eighty pounds is putting up a fight. Good for her.

I want to help. My instincts are to use my sun powers and trap him in rings of light from a tornado. But they never come. Since I was a child they never come. I try it again, as instincts would have it, feeling the power grow within. I extend out my warming hands, feeling the energy concentrate in my gut, focusing.

Caitlin looks at me with her straight blond hair and red highlights and a judging expression. "What the hell are you doing?" She shakes her head and rolls her eyes. "You are so weird."

"Oh, right, nothing," I say lowering my hands tucking them into my pockets.

Across the street, the mean lumberjack yanks the lady's bag free knocking her to the sidewalk. He takes off running down the street banging into a guy emptying garbage cans and almost upturns a baby stroller.

Caitlin yells at me again. "Now what are you doing?" I hear gasps from the older women. "What? Nothing. Oh my…" I say, looking down.

My feet are moving as if I'm jogging in place, without me *trying* to jog in place. But I do want to jog in place. Run in place. I like jogging in place, running.

I look at the women then back down at my feet. My legs pump faster. My mind switches on. I *can* run fast. I can run *very fast*.

My leg muscles twitch and thicken, filling out my pants. My lower body warms from the heat and friction. I stare at my feet in confusion then at the woman across the street. My body turns slightly to where the man is running as if my instincts are calculating his trajectory.

My knees now pump as if pistons in a car preparing to race. My body is tense, feeling the extra blood pumping through. My mind is hyper aware of the woman's every detail, wrinkles under her eyes, a tear at the bottom of her blouse, the baby stroller nearby, gum on the sidewalk. There's a man on a scaffolding, a cab driver picking his nose, a woman reading a book in a coffee shop window, pigeons on the wire, mice on top of brown paper bags chasing each other. I've never felt so alive. Physically drawn to the scene as if a wind drawing me near.

"I… I don't know what's happening," I say to the women whose eyes have grown wider than their heads. A wind is being created. The green pepper rolls off the counter and her stack of coupons blow into the air.

My pumping legs sound like a jet engine. My mind calms with this single purpose: to help. Drawn to the mugging, I feel stronger and sharper than I ever have. I feel powerful, free, alive. Woo hoo! I want to dance but can't. Must focus. Have a job to do.

Uh oh, I'm lifting off the floor. The counter is below me. "Oh God. Oh God. Excuse me. Be right *baaaa-cckk.*"

Effortlessly I fly over the counter landing at the door, a ten-foot jump. I stare, amazed, looking back at Caitlin and the green pepper lady who are equally surprised. Jaws drop.

Oh body, where have you been my whole life?

Purple Robe steps aside. With a thrust, my hand confidently pops open the screen door. In a blurring blaze I zoom across the street legs pumping feet barely touching the ground as I zigzag between cars then pedestrians down the sidewalk. I'm focused only on the woman and lumberjack.

Zipping past people like a race car driver. My feet spinning in rotations, blurring like a cartoon character. A wind of newspaper and debris swirl behind me. Cars and people appear to stand still. There's no sound other than air moving around my body and my pumping legs. I look down at my legs and get dizzy.

Never look down, I tell myself.

Looking up, I zero in on the lumberjack who's about to cross 60th.

Not gonna happen, pal.

At the crosswalk in less than a second after leaving the store I snatch the bag and zip to the far diagonal street corner weaving between cars and people, then I stop. The thief only knows the bag is gone. He looks around like a dog that's lost his bone.

Time ticks normally by again, slowing.

Mission accomplished.

Cars and people begin moving. My stomach is queasy, turning over. Walking normally, my wobbly legs have lost their rippling mass.

Did that just happen? No one gawks at me. I stop and spin around. Everyone's going about their business as usual. But I do have the lady's bag.

Worn down and sluggish I cross the street, walking toward her feeling as if I'd just run a marathon.

The lumberjack is bewildered, looking at his hands then me down the block with the bag. Cupping his hands he shouts, "Hey you, how'd you do that?"

I shrug.

"Well, where'd you come from?"

I point and say, "The store."

He purses his lips and nods as if my response is reasonable.

The woman is thankful, with tears in her eyes.

"Oh, thank you, young man. There must have been bus fumes, dear. I don't know what happened," she says, confused, as I hand her the bag. "How did you do that? I didn't see you, but you are a brave young man indeed." She smiles, pats me on the head, and walks away clutching her bag.

Puzzled, I walk back. "You were here then you had her bag over there." People say in similar confusion outside the store. "We lost you between the cars."

I reenter the store feeling pretty good, strutting a bit as I slide back behind the cash register. "Not bad, huh?" I say, leaning against the counter.

Caitlin and the two women stare. Caitlin crosses her arms, leaning against her counter then frowns, chastising me. "Well, what the hell happened to you? You tried jumping over the counter and tripped out of the store. It was *so* ridiculous." She turns back to her register, shaking her head and snapping gum.

"Wait, what? I ran after..."

Old Green Peppers says after purchasing her items, "Thank you for trying, dear. But you did get the bag. Well, after the man dropped it."

That woman's voice comes to me again: "They cannot believe what they cannot accept. It defies law. Many are prisoners of their own beliefs. Evolved ones will lift all others like a rising tide. You've done well."

Well, it's obvious their minds won't allow them to believe I moved that fast. I wouldn't believe it either. Not entirely sure I do. I remember one mystical book said, "If an event occurs outside of common norms, a mind will rewrite the experience to make an inexplicable event more palatable within an accepted reality." Or something like that.

Behind the counter I notice rashes and small holes in my arms and legs, and poke at them. The next woman in line, who always brings more coupons than money, nods. "Better take care of yourself, sweetie. Use some salve. Pimples are coming in." After I ring up a few items she asks, "How much for these Grape Nuts?"

"Three dollars and forty-nine cents."

"I'll take them," she says and sorts through her discount booklet.

I begin bagging her items then collapse on the floor.

*

When I come to, Sally, the owner, helps me up. She's thirty-something and divorced. Slim, jogger.

"I don't feel so well," I say, holding my head.

"Now that you're eighteen you're probably partying too hard. Go take a break." She nods toward the back.

On the cot I drift to a beach of black diamond glittered sand with lavender colored waters. Jintara is at my side, a seven-foot-tall warrior and my best friend.

After sleep and lunch, I'm back on my feet working again while a headache vibrates my skull. The store closes in a few hours. We're almost there as I step back in.

DEEPER IN WE FALL

I WORK THE small produce area removing wilted lettuce, sprucing up the Romaine. I grab a few apples from the walk-in cooler that feels so good I stand in there for a minute. Trying to pass the time, I uncrate more milk into the dairy fridge for people needing cereal and coffee for breakfast the next day. Checking my watch, two hours have passed. One to go. I neaten the hot and cold cereal aisle, pulling boxes forward for better presentation. Back to the register for the last half hour as things have gotten busy again. After this I'm going home to rest.

I ring up a few purchases for commuters needing a quick snack. Ten minutes to go when a dirty man opens the door surveying the room. Some strange symbol, a tattoo, rests just under his right eye. He's big, with shaggy hair, unclean. He looks like trouble with menacing black eyes and a black trench coat.

"We're closing, sir."

"Come on, little boy, I'm here for milk," he says. His coat is tattered as if from being dragged.

I nod for him to enter. The man takes a few steps in, scanning the room, when his feet and eyes stop. Staring at a tall, slender man in line who's staring back at him with blazing blue eyes. After shaking his head and breaking the trance, the tattooed man abruptly walks out, leaving the door open.

Whatever. "Next…" I say, needing the day to end fast, feeling too weak to face the world.

The tall, slender man places a single pack of gum on the counter.

I look down. "Is that it?"

"Yes," he says in a low, measured voice.

I look up and could swear this guy's eyes are glowing. He's lanky with disheveled clothes and a too-large oblong head, but his eyes are unmistakable.

He peers down at me. I quickly look away. Seeing things. I need rest. I'm weak and don't want to look him in the eyes.

"Okay, sir." I ring him up while my head aches, spins, feeling as if I might faint again.

I read the register for the price. "One, umm…" I shake my head a couple of times, staring at it. "…forty-eight. One forty-eight." I don't look at the tall man, but know he's looking at me.

He leans in a little. "Iron core crystals," he says then leans back out.

"I'm sorry. What?"

He speaks as if his words are dense, alive, entering my body. "You need iron core crystals if you're not well."

Startled, I abruptly look up. "How do you…?"

He nods, pays with exact change, no bills, and walks out.

*

Outside, after locking up with Sally and Caitlin, I head uptown as they walk to the train station. Half a block up I squint, staring at something across the street. I peer at what looks like a ball of smoke traveling above the sidewalk. It stops. With no eyes, it seems to face me then floats quickly down into a sewer grate. Confused, I glare closer. That must have been bus fumes or furnace exhaust.

About to step again, I notice another one floating down an alley. I feel faint, chills, with a lump in my throat.

I might need to get my head examined. It's true. Must get home to rest. Looking around I don't see anything else and quicken my pace.

At home I lock the deadbolt, chain, and am so stirred up I sit on my bed trying to calm my thoughts, slowing my breath with meditation, but my mind spins. I open my book but immediately close it. Thoughts bubble up. I ran super-fast, man with weird blue eyes spoke to me, another man with symbol under eye wanted something, and then there were floating exhaust blobs. I definitely need to call Dr. G.

Restless, pacing the apartment not knowing where to put this information, I draw the blinds and microwave a chicken pot pie. Sitting at my desk eating, I look up the weird tattoo on my laptop. After a few minutes of scanning the vast array of tattoos on the Internet, some elaborately cool with incredible artwork, and some not so much.

I find it on page twelve of my search. The fork stops at my mouth. It's the symbol of a devilish sect stemming back to ancient Mesopotamia, believing in day's end.

The worlds *are* converging. "Day's end," I say aloud.

I finish eating deep in thought, wondering what the heck it all means. And I have no idea. Then what did that other weird guy say? Oh right. "Iron core crystals." He said it with such dramatic effect, like he was in some bad movie. I type that into the search bar.

"Earth's inner core is made of a nickel-iron alloy. The solid inner core of Earth is iron. It is surrounded by a liquid outer core composed of nickel-iron alloy. Only recently has it been discovered that iron crystals at the center of the earth are thought by mystics to contain great healing properties. But access to these crystals are limited and can only be found on the black market and secret government labs."

I stumble to bed and fall asleep, dizzy from the day. Like I'm falling down a never-ending well. I close my eyes tight and cover my head with a pillow. The city doesn't know that the world is ripping in two. That I am. Not sure it would care.

BUMPING AGAINST THE SINISTER

I WAKE DRENCHED in sweat hearing a banging sound from the fire escape as if heavy paint cans are being dragged step by step. On edge, I bounce up, peering out. There's nothing but exhaust fumes from a garbage truck below. It's still dark. I lie in bed, eyes open, mind alert. Body tired.

The next morning is quiet at work. Everything's normal. The sun is shining with that strange rusted hue I've gotten used to. People commute. Cabs honk. Food truck vendors sit near the subway entrance. I overhear conversations about baseball and vacations to beach resorts. Perhaps I bumped my head and, well… dreamt it all.

At the store I stock produce and shelves. A couple hours later I work at the register and neaten the counter items. I take lunch and sit outside feeding pigeons pieces of my multigrain bread from a turkey and swiss sandwich. Things are in place. Normal.

I people watch. There's a unicyclist going up the wrong way on Vexington, a small woman walks eight dogs, and Chinese delivery men on bicycles deliver food to office buildings. I sit on the low wall of a fountain with the sun on my head. All is well. All is all it should be. I don't hear any arguments.

The start of the afternoon work is equally pleasant. I grab boxes of cinnamon granola from the stock room for a nice lady who needs extra for visiting relatives and their children. While handing them to her, my little buddy Dino runs up the aisle full speed into my stomach. Upph. He and his sister Laurie-Ann live up the block and visit often.

"Reuben!" he shouts, hugging me tight. He's a sweet kid with brown shaggy hair, a round head, and chubby cheeks.

His sister walks up the aisle smiling. "Hey, Reuben."

"Hi Laurie-Ann, how are you?" She can't be much more than my age.

"Not as well as him," she says, smiling. She's pretty, with straight teeth.

"How are you, Dino?" I ask, looking down. He squeezes me harder. He can't be older than five or six.

"Dino, don't kill him," Laurie-Ann says jokingly.

They come in every few days. I've never seen a father or mother for that matter. Laurie-Ann's always friendly. Her stares linger. Her blond hair is long and straight. Her blue eyes smile like the sky.

"You remind me of someone," I say again.

"I know, Reuben. You always tell me that. But who? Like an aunt?"

I shake my head and shrug. "Don't know. Just familiar. It's a good thing."

She makes a sour face and scrunches her eyes. "You're so weird…" she says but stares longer.

From behind me I hear, "Excuse me, sir. Sir? Are you working or on break?"

I turn, and the interrupting woman is a short middle-aged troll with many creases on her face and too much makeup.

"Well, are you working or not, hmm?" She steps closer, too close. I back up almost into the cereal shelf.

"I'm working, but you interrupted the conversation I was having with these costumers."

She looks at them behind me. "I don't see them buying anything."

Laurie-Ann chuckles. "It's okay, Reuben. We'll catch you later." Laurie-Ann makes another sour face and crosses her eyes. I smile.

"Bye, Reuben."

"See ya, buddy."

They turn, hold hands, and walk out.

"Okay, so what can I do for you?" I clap my hands together patiently trying not to jump down her throat.

The lady has menacing red eyes and mutters to herself in a language I've never heard, and this being a diverse neighborhood, I've heard many.

"I must buy something," she says.

"Okay, this is a fun game."

She hands me money in the aisle.

"Well, what are you buying?"

She places a finger to her lips and wanders off.

With money in hand I walk over to the register and watch her. She walks into the next aisle where two of the sweetest women shop together. They've been best friends for over forty years and have shopped together once a week for all that time.

She bumps one of them and blames the woman. "Watch where you're going, missy!"

I shake my head. There's no shortage of rude people. She walks over, placing a spatula on the counter.

"That's it?" It seems such a strange purchase, and not an emergency.

"Yes, this is what I need."

"Okay." I shake my head, picking it up to read the price on the bottom when she grabs my hands tightly in hers then closes her eyes, speaking in this muttering language. *"Bruntdndn, bruntdndn, lashevan, lashevan, bruntdndn, bruntdndn.mmnmnmnmn, rstlan, rstlan, mnmnmnmnnnnnn, bruntdndn, bruntdndn."* She releases my hands, opens her eyes, then scowls at me, twisting her mouth to the side.

Regaining my composure, I ask, "Why did you do that?" I hand her back her change tucking my hands into my pocket. She walks out without a word, leaving the spatula behind.

In the aisle the women begin arguing. "Well, your husband was never that bright… God rest his soul… and the chicken breast you make is always dry… I'm shopping elsewhere and without *you…*"

The one woman puts down her basket and walks out. The other woman, Dolores, stands in shock. "Well, good riddance," she says with tears in her eyes.

I look back at the woman who just left, knowing she had something to do with this.

SEEING IS NOT BELIEVING

ON MY WAY home after closing an old man comes out of a bank clutching his money when a smoke ball descends over him. The old man scowls. His hands wave as if swatting away mosquitoes as he disappears into the expanding fog.

My feet involuntarily shift forward, my knees pump, drawn to the cloud like salmon are drawn upstream. The cloud grows larger as more fuzzy smoke balls the size of basketballs dart in, expanding it. Pedestrians walk past. No one seems to notice.

I hustle over and enter the haze cloud. Disoriented at first, ready to pump knees and grab the man to safety. Yet the air is heavy, sulfuric, and I can't see well. Bodiless forms swoop and gnaw on him, attacking with horns and fangs, darting through him effortlessly. I wonder who this old man is and what he did. Disfigured creatures with distorted eyes like from my night terrors seize upon him. Though sweating, I shiver and feel weak.

Taking notice, they release him to swarm around me. They bite and slash. My thoughts shift to negative ones, not feeling powerful at all. The man falls to the ground bleeding, with money in his hand, tears in his eyes.

I can't stop them with fists that land on nothing. There are too many and they are increasing. My knees have stopped pumping. I have no speed or powers, growing feebler as an illness takes over. I feel my head, growing sad thinking about my parents and how they died. I could have saved them. I was so useless. What is the point of my life? My parents wondered if I was even theirs. Unwanted memories from kids in school who made fun of me and beat me up because I was different.

The car accident and death of my parents plays over and over again. I hear the crashing, screams, and bending metal.

Dreams that haunt me. Our kingdom and the dark blades of mist killing everyone. I am so lost, lonely. Cold.

Death pulls me to join them, surrender to the pain. Tears of sadness run down my cheeks as I fall to the ground curling up like a baby. The entities dive and dart around me.

More haze expands the black cloud as a storm rains inside me. Sadness consumes me as they gnaw on my life. I can't fight them. I deserve them. Anger turns inward at how bad I've been. I hate who I am. How I look, where I work, that I've caused so much trouble.

Wanting them to end me. I'm curled in a blubbering ball while my family is murdered again and again. I want to close my eyes forever when I see large sneakers and bony legs beside me. Expecting them to stomp and put me out of my misery, I grab at the legs. "Please... Please. Do it now." All of my pain rises.

I follow the legs. It's the tall thin man with the blue eyes standing inside the storm. I should've known he was trouble. I close my eyes briefly, waiting for it to end. But no foot comes stomping down.

Opening my eyes, I see him swinging his arms wildly. His blazing blue eyes shine like a spotlight, hitting these scary entities, which dry up and disappear. He jumps around like a lunatic and the cloud grows lighter. They cower as he faces them. They flee, scatter, and the cloud is gone as if blown away by wind.

I'm now laying on the sidewalk a few feet from the old man. The thin man helps him up and brushes him off as he scampers away, still holding his money. "Thank you," he mutters.

The day returns and people walk by. Many glance at me, shaking their heads.

"Look at him. Just lying on the sidewalk. I am so sick of bums," one man says.

Painful memories fade and the tears stop. The thin man pulls me up as other pedestrians pass by, disinterested.

*

He brushes me off. "You should be more careful now that you're eighteen." He scans up and down the block then grabs me, pulling me in close. His eyes penetrate and his voice speaks firmly. "That was a trap and you did not know. Why?"

I shake my head, confused.

"They lured you."

"What are those creatures? I don't know what you're asking me."

"Those are trapped entities, prisoners if you will, that believe if they kill you, they will be freed. But they are mistaken. They will only find more pain."

He releases me. "How do you get like that?"

"Toxins in their blood tapping into their most base emotions: fear, pain, loss. The essence of each soul is trapped by the dark forces. They cannot be in their bodies or continue their evolutionary journey until they can free themselves.

"Oh." I nod. This guy is nuts.

He turns and walks away. "Come," he says over his shoulder without looking back. "You have been trapped as well, between two worlds."

I hear his words while watching more haze balls gather above sewer grates and outside building ducts.

STRANGE APARTMENT

INSIDE HIS APARTMENT, there are stacks of food boxes and junk in all directions. I wonder if this guy's a hoarder. Sunlight fans in with the shades drawn. Complex math problems float in front of the walls and ceiling. They glow blue and move in wavelike motion. The numbers in one equation keep changing, updating. I glance around for a projector. Gross, he uses the kitchen sink for washing his clothes. Laundry hangs above food crusted dishes hanging from cabinet doors.

"They did invent washing mach—"

"Shh, do not speak." He listens at a wall, leaning through one equation that shifts out of his way. He places his ear over to the front door then checks the three deadbolts. He strides to the middle of the room, straightening his back, raising his chin, and stops. His blues eyes match the hue of the projections. "I am Tanz the Accountant," he says matter-of-factly.

I almost burst out laughing. "You're an accountant?"

He nods proudly.

"That was some badass stuff out there for an accountant. But, uh, I don't need my taxes done. Excellent customer service, however. You saved me and I do appreciate that. Nice place you've got." I step to leave, reaching for the door.

"Boy, sit down." He points to a cloth chair with books, shirts, and plates on it. I stare, not wanting to. He sighs, moving the items. "Sorry, not used to guests. Now, where was I?"

I shrug, sitting without leaning back, not wanting to stick to anything.

"To mortals, I am a seer."

I nod, he should *see* how he lives.

"Clearly by that vacant look in your eyes you do not understand. I account for events before, during, and after they have happened, every detail, even the most minute, something off in the shadows, I can and will observe."

He raises both hands. Blue streaks come alive leaving trails behind them like airplane exhaust. The equations pulsate and thump.

"I hope your landlord doesn't mind."

He ignores me as images play from the event outside: me leaving the store then into the haze cloud, then the gnawing and suffering. I remember the pain.

Leaning forward I ask, "How do you do that?" I scan the room for a camera. "This must be one of those gotcha shows." Yet upon seeing the mess, I realize no one would film here.

"Shh, do not speak. Your brain must relearn who you are. These immature quips achieve nothing."

"Sorry, I crack jokes when I get nervous. My psychiatrist says it's a coping mechanism."

He strides to the window and peers out. "Time is limited. Your life is in danger. Any jokes now?" He glances over his shoulder at me.

"No, I'm sorry. But this is too much. Too much is happening I don't understand. I don't know who I am or why I'm here or what the heck is going on."

Pondering, he returns to the room's center. "You are a very powerful young man. More powerful than your mind can currently fathom. You were hidden from the dark forces by the sun gods after our de-evolution and Narican's fall. You have always sensed more exists beyond what your eyes can see, yet you have never arrived at this broader self."

I nod absently. He is a seer. "I've always felt like an outsider looking in."

"Indeed, you are. We were deceived by the dark forces."

"Dark forces, sir?"

He nods.

"Besides sunlight illuminating and encouraging life to grow, there is an equal and opposite dark light. And this dark light or dark force illuminates only suffering, pain, and destruction of all that lives. It is the very opposite of love, goodness, and devotion. And against the code of Narican to live at one's highest state. Let me ask: do you dream?"

"Sure. Who doesn't?"

"And what do you dream of?"

"I... I'd rather not say. I need to call my doctor." I stand, wanting to leave.

He clasps his hands together. "A great battle, perhaps? Your father, a king, being cut down by a dark blade of mist?"

"How do you know that?"

"I am the record keeper. I was there. Your dreams are not dreams at all, yet past life recollections trapped within your cells. They are your memories," he says, pointing at my chest.

I sit again, reaching for the dirty chair, and lean back. "How do you know these things?"

"Do you know of the Akashic Records?"

I shake my head.

With patience he continues, "The Akashic Records have recorded every thought and moment in universal history. It is a database of all histories, not only Earth's, but all realms, precincts, dimensions. I created them and yet our families were murdered or cast out into the universe. There are no records as to how or why."

I shake my head and shrug. "Aka... what? So, you're a record producer and an accountant? I'm not really following you. We were cast out? Is that why I have these dreams? You realize I work at a grocery store and have no idea what you're talking about. I can help you with yams and rhubarb."

"I understand it is a process. Allow your mind to expand."

I take a deep breath. "Okay, so how did these bad guys avoid these records of yours?"

"That is something we must find out. They are here now, infiltrating this planet. And if we do not find them, it will fall. Your family kept these dark forces, this dark light at bay the way a body's immune system keeps bacteria in check. That is how the universe remained balanced. Now that is lost. I have scanned the records and no information has been recorded."

"Like it's been deleted?"

"No, impossible. More as if it was never there, which is equally impossible. You must remember who you are. It is imperative," he says, pointing at me with a long slender finger again, "Claremone."

I bolt upright. "Wait, how do you know my *name?*"

"I know much about you."

"Well, why don't I know you?"

"There had been no need until now. And you were just a boy."

Tanz turns back to his calculations. They shimmer with a blue radiance as if alive. As he completes each one it collapses and flies off.

"Here, let me show you." In a flurry of movement, he shows a planet that sits atop a funnel tornado.

"These are the dimensions. The bottom one for sentient beings is here, Earth." The depiction moves and sways with his blue life force. "This is Narican, our home."

I reach out to touch it. He zooms into the planet, past the atmosphere and black triangle mountains and diamond palaces that sparkle within mountainsides; waterfalls of lavender run alongside, and all sit under three onyx moons.

"This is Narican now."

Black clouds fill the horizon; broken, collapsing buildings; people enslaved, doing menial labor removing boulders with vacant looks in their eyes, suffering.

He turns to me. "Do you understand who your dream family is?"

I shake my head. "Not really."

"You and I are the last of the Sun Clan, the gatekeeper to the gods that reside within each star, including the sun of this planet. The peace had been kept for millennia. With the cleansing we were betrayed by the Toxic Whisperers, and reduced to human form, the lowest form of sentient being."

"Wait, wait, wait, slow down. Reduced to human form? Cleansing? What are you talking about?"

"The toxins that spread on Narican are the same toxins spreading here. They devolve or kill organisms depending upon quantity intake. The dark forces use it as a weapon. That storm is sweeping through the dimensions."

"How? What does it do?"

"The toxins sever DNA strands, functions."

I nod, trying to allow this information in. My brain hurts but somehow

I understand. "You mentioned the sun. Is that why it's turned rust colored?"

Tanz peers out the blinds. "Yes." But offers nothing further.

"Well, how do we stop them? Do they fear? I mean, what's their weakness?"

"They hide with bravado, loud chatter, safety in numbers, manipulation. Only a Light Being can dissipate them, like a morning sun evaporates fog. That is why they scattered when I stared into them. Their fears and doubts defeated them, not I. The extent of my warrior powers are to be but a mirror.

"Many humans are torn in two between their emotions and spirit. It is the great dichotomy, the great struggle of higher and lower self. Wanting to be more, while stuck in pain. I look out this window and see the daily struggle. Feeling they are more than their daily lives present, their true lives somewhere off in the distance. Only the alignment can bring these two sides together."

I nod, knowing exactly what he means.

"May I read your memories?"

I nod.

"Please stand."

He places his hands over my forehead and stomach.

"Your center is the soul or spiritual cavity and your link to the past and universe."

Ah, the *dantian*, I think but don't say. "So, we've lived before?" I ask as he approaches.

"Yes."

"Is that why people say I'm an old soul?"

He chuckles, nodding. "I'd say, approximately 2.2 million years. Now, quiet your mind," he says, placing his hands on me. It feels as if I've exploded and someone dived inside my skin.

He speaks in low measured tones. "You were born here through a surrogate yet lived during the great battle before the cleansing. You were not killed as they could not catch you because of your speed. At the time of your cleansing and severing of DNA, Jan and Robert Mitchell were conceiving."

"But why them?"

"A benevolent protective yoke. Their love would keep you safe."

Tanz breaks the connection. "There is nothing I don't already know." He looks at the rashes and holes in my skin. "Let me find you some iron crystals," he says walking into another room then returning with a container.

"These will balance out your vibrational energy and undo the cleansing. You will heal in time and align. That inner being you sense will develop and come to fruition."

He looks at the wall and the blue numbers updating. "Thermostatic pressure has shifted. You must leave." He peeks out the window. "It is not safe now." He pulls me up and hurries me to the door.

"They are gathering and will soon strike, tracking our markers."

I brush his hand off. "Are they stronger than us?"

"The dark forces are ubiquitous but individually weak. Their energy disperses when truth is revealed or the light of one's true self shines upon them."

I cross my arms. "I'm not leaving until you tell me what happened to my parents. My Earth parents."

Annoyed, he lets out a heavy sigh. "They are not relevant."

"They're relevant to me. They're my parents."

Tanz brings up the image of shadows closing in around the car then wipes it away. "They were murdered to get to you. After the seventeenth revolution around Earth's sun they can attack the surrogate family directly if previously unsuccessful in eliminating its offspring. There are laws even the dark light cannot defy."

"They killed them just like that?" I sit down on a nearby chair and look up with tears dropping from my eyes. "Because of me?"

"Mourning is acceptable, a cleansing of sorts."

After wiping my eyes and sniffling I say, "There's no time for mourning. They're here and we must stop them. My parents were good people."

"If we do not act soon there won't be any good people left. Their minds will be altered and their memories twisted into anger, pain, and darkness as the Toxic Whisperers corrupt and disconnect them from their higher selves."

"Like how I felt outside?"

He nods. "Violence and destruction will consume them. Their demeanor will be altered indelibly, and this planet will be condemned by the higher ranks so not to infect the universe."

"But where *aren't* the dark forces?"

"In pure hearts."

"Like babies?"

"Yes, but in others as well. Babies are too young to help."

"I guess we have to find them."

Tanz nods.

"But how?"

"They will come to us. Like attracts like. Cells bond with similar cells."

"But how will I know who the dark forces are?"

"They will come as friends, dark mist, haze, fumes, light disruptions, anger, confusion, and can take over bodies for short periods of time," he says, opening the door and shoving me into the hall. "Anyway the Toxic Whisperers can get to you."

I hear those last words as the door slams and deadbolts snap. In the hall I'm alone looking at chipping paint and uneven floors. Though I'm overloaded, I feel my consciousness opening, like I'm becoming Claremone, seeing a little clearer.

I'm careful going home. Outside I see nothing. But after a few steps I hear my name in mocking tones echoing off buildings. "Clar-eee-mone… Clar-eee-mone… Your time is coming. Just like your family."

I want to stop and fight, swing fists into the air but there's nothing, no one.

In my apartment, exhausted from events and information overload, I sleep like the dead. This night is dreamless yet whispers from beyond enter my mind carrying words.

"They are coming for you, child. Prepare yourself. Know that you are loved."

ONE WEIRD MORNING

BEFORE I FULLY wake, as dawn creeps toward me, I hear my name called again.

"Clar-eee-mone." The voice drifts up from the alley behind my building.

Ready to do battle I jump out of bed and look out the window.

The voice fades with distance. *"Clar-eee-mone..."*

A sliver of a rusty sun cracks over the city's buildings.

As I get ready for work, that female's voice speaks in my head, *"Trust Tanz. He is a family ally."*

Outside, people on the sidewalk act strange. Well, stranger than usual. Everyone is scowling. One woman walks into me and yells, "Watch where you're walking, buster!" Then she mutters something to herself.

In line at the shop people yell at each other about who got there first. Canned goods and cereal boxes lay in the aisles.

At the register, Caitlin asks, "Are people getting weirder?"

I ask her, "What's with the stuff on the floor?"

She shrugs. "Like that when I got here. Sally opened."

Another female coworker, Jen, walks past. "Mercury must be in retrograde."

I don't know what that means and don't want to risk sounding stupid. I pick up the food from the aisles and restock it.

Out the shop window I see a dark haze envelope a walking man. His face turns to anger. He kicks at a plastic bag in front of him then trounces down the street like an angry bulldozer with shoulders shifted forward.

"Reuben, can you come in the back?" the store owner, Sally, shouts from an open door at the rear.

She has a small office with lots of shelving and a desk stacked with paper. A folding chair sits in front. A door to the supply room stands closed along the side wall.

"I think it's time we celebrate, Reuben. The store has been doing so well, thanks to you. Because of your outstanding service, I'm increasing your pay five dollars an hour and making you a supervisor."

"Wow, Sally, I don't know what to say."

"Well, say yes, silly!"

"Jen and Caitlin also do great jobs. But wow, a five-dollar raise is huge."

She reaches out her hand to shake. I take it and it seems stronger than usual.

A container of my favorite all-natural apple juice sits on her desk with two cups already poured. "Let's celebrate with a healthy toast."

"I do love this juice," I say, gazing at it.

"I know. It's irresistible." Her voice sounds strange, as if she has a cold.

"Are you feeling okay?"

She nods, picking up her cup to drink.

She sips, smacking her lips. "Hmm, delicious. Now your turn."

I pick mine up and watch it bubble, feeling chills in my bones.

"Don't get jittery now. It's your favorite. Besides a five dollar raise is a lot of money for an eighteen-year-old. You could move out of that little apartment or ask one of the girls out. Or the sister of that boy who comes in here. I see how she looks at you."

I lower my cup hand. Something doesn't feel right.

"Um, I'm not thirsty. I just had a drink," I say, shrugging to the store. "But I'll take the raise."

I notice a red glint in her eyes: something harsh and loveless.

"That's very rude, Claremone." Her voice drops further.

"Wait, how do you know my...?"

She aggressively yanks my hand across her desk. *"Drink, boy!"* A man's voice barrels out. And she—he—tries to force me.

"No!" I shout, struggling.

Butch, the burly supply room worker, enters from the side door.

"Hold him!"

I can't create rings of light or defend myself with any powers. I struggle as Sally walks around the desk with the cup. Butch holds me down. He too has red in his eyes. The bubbling liquid gets closer. I'm trapped but keep envisioning my power. Nothing comes.

I must fight. My boss is about to pour poison down my throat. I look around then kick the folding chair that knocks the cup into a metal filing cabinet. The liquid spills out, sizzling, eating a hole in the metal. I ram Butch into the wall behind us as shelves and heavy books tumble down upon him. I step on Butch's foot, elbow him, and escape out the door.

"Get him!" Sally shouts while my legs pump. I'm moving faster.

I run past Jen and Caitlin at the register and out the front door. I hear Jen's voice as the door is closing. "Yup, people are definitely getting weirder."

Caitlin says, "And what's with Sally? Sounds like a guy I used to date."

They laugh as I scoot up the block.

FLEEING WITH TANZ

OUT OF BREATH, I get to his apartment and bang on the door.

"Tanz, it's me. It's me. Let me in!" I shout.

The deadbolts unlock and the door opens. Tanz's head pops out, checking all angles of the hall and staircase. His eyes move like camera lenses zooming in and out.

"Come. Come," he says, yanking me into the room and slamming the door behind me, locking it.

"It has begun. The epic battle of good and evil," he says, shoulders back, as he looks off into the distance.

"Um, Tanz, I'm right here."

"Yes, yes. Too many old movies."

I begin pacing past the glowing equations to the drawn blinds and back.

"How did they get inside my boss?"

"If sorrow, regret, negative opinions, surface in one's mind, they can enter through these channels. They penetrate and prey upon the weakened state and uncertain parts of one's psyche."

"Now I understand everything growing up—" I say in disgust—"the lawnmower, the falling street sign, all of it. My whole life. Is nothing real?"

"Breathing deep roots us. Breathe...It is all real, Claremone. Everything you have felt and experienced. Your name does not define you. Actions do. Abilities. Your commitments. May I?" He raises his hands and places them on me. He replays the fight in Sally's office. "Hmm," is all he says.

He stops the scene and points. "Here. There is a red glint in her eyes. Pay attention to these signals: facial tics, tricks of light, strange events, inconsistencies… they will guide your movements and reactions. You have done well. Now we must flee."

"Flee?"

"Yes. We need more information and they know where we are. Their trackers will soon be upon us."

"Grab a few things and meet me back here at noon. Much is at stake. The sun will be overhead and will cast the fewest shadows for them to hide within. Events are all based on universal timing. One minute too early or late changes the fate of things and their outcome." He creates a calculation on the wall and we watch it countdown: 3, 2, 1—it closes then flies off. "Now is our opportunity. *Go!*" He commands.

Down the stairs I fly hearing the deadbolts latch behind me. Two blocks over to my building, I hoof it up the five flights two steps at time.

Inside my apartment I grab a backpack, clothes, essentials, my parents' picture.

Skipping back down I make it to the sidewalk. Outside my building Dino is walking down the street with his sister.

"Reuben!" He runs over and hugs me. But I'm not sure if I can trust them so step off a few feet.

His sister Laurie-Ann approaches asking, "Aren't you working today? We were coming to visit."

"No, I guess I'm not. Going on a little trip."

"Where to?"

"Um, not sure." I break eye contact with her.

She nods and jokes, "Sounds well planned out…"

"I'm sorry, but I have to go. Stay outta trouble, champ."

"Bye, Reuben," Dino says, sweet little guy.

"Bye, Laurie-Ann," I say and run off, double checking they aren't following me. Only standing there with quizzical looks.

Back at his building, I don't see Tanz but a guy in a leather jacket revving a red motorcycle with black hard cases. I cautiously move closer. Too quiet. No cabs around. Nobody's shouting. The bike revs louder and there's no sign of Tanz anywhere. Did they get him? I cling close to the brick building when a woman with a poodle walks out the front door. She doesn't see me.

"Come on, Mitzy. Don't take too long now. Mama has a hair appointment." She says as they walk in the other direction.

The bike revs louder and the rider waves me over. "Let's go! What are you waiting for?" He flips the helmet visor up. It's Tanz on the motorcycle.

I edge closer. "I didn't know you rode—"

"I don't. Now get on."

"Well, where did you get it?"

"Stole it…" he says as I step on the foot peg and swing my leg over.

He hands me a helmet. "I thought you needed a pure heart." I ask, slipping it over my head.

"*You* do," he says, jamming it into gear then full throttle popping a wheelie down the block. "But also, necessary *meee-aaa-nnnnn-ssss.*" I almost fly off but hold on tight.

As we lean into turns and around cars, Tanz waves his left hand, showing me images of him hot wiring the bike and reading the riding manual. He throttles the machine relentlessly with his right hand. Full speed in third gear now fourth, he's clearly having a blast. In the mirror I see a smile plastered on his face.

"Accounting is *fuuuunnnnn,*" he says.

I'm terrified holding on. The speedometer reads eighty-seven miles per hour and the needle is jumping as we weave through traffic.

"Red light. Red light! *Red light!*" I shout, bracing for impact into a black sedan.

He shifts around a double-parked limousine and rides up onto the sidewalk then takes a sharp right turn into a park. Pigeons fly off. He's nuts!

"You're going to kill us!" I say, adrenaline pumping, nerves shattering. My ears throb from the engine noise as my head bounces along.

"Shortest distance is a straight line."

Now a traffic cops pursues us as Tanz runs a red light. They get stuck as we turn the corner and hop onto the highway entrance ramp doing a hundred and ten and climbing. The tachometer shakes at ten thousand rpm, just under the redline as we zoom out of the city.

We ride upstate full speed for two hours into the Bears Kill Mountains. Pulling into an empty campground just before dusk. My legs are wobbly as we dismount. Taking off my helmet, I shout, "You're going to kill us before the dark forces can!"

"I will have you know, every turn, speed, tire thread, even the wind velocity was calculated for. No jeopardy were we in at all." He breathes deeply, placing his helmet over the bike mirror. "Oh, what wonderful forest air." He breathes deeply again, filling his lungs.

"Well, what about squirrels and branches on the road, did you calculate for that?"

Tanz falls silent; his smile turns to alarm.

"Well, you got us here," I say, slapping his shoulder then sitting on the picnic table.

Without words he unpacks the hard case and throws me a sleeping bag and tent. I drop my backpack on the ground and begin setting up.

After the tent is set and sleeping bags laid inside, I search for firewood. "This is the first time I've been to a state park since the accident," I say, walking off.

Tanz understands with knowing eyes. He sets food on the picnic table and unwraps a dinner of turkey and broccoli with nice silverware and paper plates. Napkins set properly under the fork and knife.

Returning with wood, the meal seems strange and elaborate for a campground. "Turkey and broccoli, huh?" I say, stopping in front.

"Yes, I saw it on a cooking show. Very healthy." There's an image of Tanz with a baker's hat wearing a white and blue striped apron watching the show. "Just add a smidge of olive oil and garlic…" he says, smiling, clearly proud of himself.

I make the fire, starting with teepee style and pine needles underneath to get a base and quick flame. We eat in quiet in front of the campfire. The night is dark as the campfire illuminates us.

"Why did we come here and not go to a motel?" I ask, poking at the fire.

"There is a natural protective buffer here from the dark forces. Nature is inherently aligned with light and balance. This is why people meditate in the woods, find peace and rehabilitation at a waterfall. The gods set it up this way." He cuts into his turkey and broccoli then properly places the knife along plate's edge.

"A sanctuary?"

"Hmm, delicious. Yes, this is also why the dark forces cut down trees and woodlands at an alarming rate." He shows this image of bald hillsides and clear-cuts, trees falling into rivers.

"Tell me more about the cleansing. How does it work and how do we undo it?"

"Well, to tell you about the cleansing I must first tell you about human history. In fact, there were two cleansings millions of years apart. So, to tell you about one I must first tell you about the other. An unusual campfire story to be sure." He pauses. "I am sorry about your parents, Claremone."

"Thank you. The turkey is delicious."

SENTIENT BEING WAR AND
THEIR SENTENCE

"There was a great war on another planet between higher and lower forms. This lower form attempted to subjugate with deception and murder, instead of evolving naturally over time. This universal history *can* be found in the records."

Confused, I ask, "What do you mean war—on another planet? I've never heard of that."

He chuckles. "No, I'd imagine you would not have. Earth had no humans then." He waves his hand to demonstrate with images. "It was lush, with waving foliage and pristine oceans. Beauty abounded without cities or sentient beings. It was a balanced world without dominion and its ecosystem worked harmoniously.

"Have you ever wondered why humans aren't in balance with the food chain? Because they are not from it. They're not at the top of the chain, either, as they like to believe. Humans are in fact imprisoned entities from this planet here." He points to a dot in a distant solar system. "As a sentence they were devolved and sent here."

I was lost but totally fascinated. This was not the history they taught us in school. "What do you mean 'devolved'?"

"Their sentence, as per universal code NC11488, Naricanian chapter, was to be stripped of DNA, unplugged, and disconnected. Strands of their higher evolutionary abilities, such as extra sensory perception and telepathy, were eliminated, energetically cut away through their sentencing. Similar to shutting off the lights in a house. They were provided the same toxins that are here now.

"On Narican there are thirty-five chakra or energy chambers. On Earth there are seven. Each one represents an awareness, an ability that a specific DNA strand handles: motor function, predispositions, eye colors, insight, concepts, ESP as mentioned, flight, accounting… everything that makes up a person's traits and abilities."

He shows this devolution and energy centers going dark within a body.

"So, if you strip certain DNA functions by shutting them off, a person may look the same, yet be forever changed.

"The war council—" he shows several levitating beings—"chose Earth as the most sensible planet for lower sentient beings. It was an oasis, a chance to start anew."

He shows them tumbling through space within a moment's time as if through a vacuum hose.

"These lower beings evolved into the ape. That is why certain apes evolved into humans and others did not.

"You're staring at me with that vacant look again."

This is so beyond me. I simply nod.

"In simpler terms, clouds pull away after an afternoon rain, yes? During the rainstorm one cannot see very far. Yet on the sunny day that follows, one can see to the horizon."

"Are you saying most humans live in that cloud where they cannot see far, but feel?"

He nods.

"My dad used to tell me to get my head out of the clouds."

"Yes, that is one way of saying it. Most humans live dualistic lives in a daily battle between their minds and souls. Within the soul of every person is a locked pulsation of that individual's truth and higher self to guide them, while the mind only knows experience, often trapping them in doubts and fears. This is where the dark forces and cleansing comes in. The cleansing manipulates and distorts one's truth, making them susceptible to suggestion and pain.

"The humans of today are failing. Just look at their cities and culture: greed, ignorance, waste, working longer hours for less."

He shows people on couches watching television like zombies.

"Slaves to their own invention. If I was a betting man—" he smiles wryly—"I would bet against them."

"There are good people, Tanz. My friend Caesar for one."

"This sentence is an opportunity. Their chance to evolve and ascend. Either they will learn or perish." Tanz is harsh and cold. "With the poisoning of their environment, they are the only species to ever destroy their own habitat." He shakes his head in disbelief. "They are helping their extinction along."

My head's hurting from information overload. After a few seconds I ask, "How did you learn to ride like that, anyway?"

He brightens up at the subject. "Well, motocross on CBS Sundays, of course."

"Of course," I say. "Well, I'm glad you didn't watch those crazy monster truck rallies."

He nods, falling silent to work on a small equation.

"We are missing pieces." The words "70% Complete" hover over an equation that he wipes away. "In conclusion, the cleansing was so successful with humans they attempted it recently on Narican, but they did not factor in the DNA of the Sun Clan with better immune system and pure blood. Thus, the cleansing of Naricanians only worked to a point…" He slows his words… "And could only work to a point, temporarily." This idea vexes him. "They would have known this…" He adds quietly to himself and adds this information to his equation like dropping keys into a drawer.

"73% Complete."

NARICAN AND THE SUN CLAN

"Tell me about Narican and the battle."

"We were not prepared. It was a surprise attack, yet I see nothing leading up to…" Tanz looks at the imagery again. The dark forces coming into the castle through vents, windows, up through the flooring like smoke. Everywhere. It's dark. He's running among others with a pregnant woman at his side. "I cannot see what I should have seen."

"It's not your fault."

"I am the accountant to the Sun Clan. We are the gate keepers."

"Gate keepers to what?" I ask.

"The gods of light that illuminate this entire universe. We protect a path from Earth to Narican for souls to evolve. And the gods of light illuminate that path.

"The cleansing was also a cleansing of us from our planet, our positions, abilities, and connections to the gods, who are now equally disconnected, growing blind. Even the spirit of our planet is cloaked. I fear Narican will grow dark as the beacon of universal light and we will all go blind. Hope will dissolve into chaos as if there is no lighthouse during a dark night at sea. As it now stands, we are homeless and godless… There is more to this attack and more at stake than meets the eye…"

"Do you think that's connected to what's going on here with the dark forces?"

"There could very well be this connection you speak of."

He brings up images of the battle scenes and runs through them again.

"We're still trying to figure out where they came from and how. They murdered who they could then grew impatient here, spraying their toxin and leaving. But the real question is how did they get there and what was their entry point?"

"Is anything happening... universally?" I ask trying to sound smarter than I feel.

"The universe is expanding. What will take humans millions of years to overcome will take us months, years, depending upon the amount of toxin absorbed into our cells and the iron crystals we can consume. They would have known this too. All of this. There is something or someone very menacing behind these events.

"Here is a known fact: water, no matter how diluted it becomes, or chemicals it is blended with, through natural processes of evaporation, will always return to being pure water. It is the only substance in the universe that has this trait. That and the blood of the Sun Clan."

He stops the image of a toxic blade and walks up to it. "These blades disintegrate life forms," he says, stoking the fire, "like burned wood to ash."

"Well, why is this now happening on Earth? A strange coincidence?"

"There are parallels, intersections, actions and reactions, never coincidence. All is interwoven. Not even the gods can avoid this fact... There's more I must tell you in case I am struck down... You must protect the innocent light of hope... It is the human's only chance of finding their way out of this darkness. Within hope there is an idea, a belief to move forward and live better. Without hope and morals to guide them humanity will be lost in eternal darkness. That is what the dark forces seek out and prey upon."

"Didn't you say something similar about eternal darkness if Narican is lost?"

He nods with a pensive expression. "You are Narican Sun Clan, the highest honor a soul can have. A warrior soul, it is our oath and duty."

I nod, taking this in. "Like what happened with the purse snatcher? My legs started moving and pumping like a wind pulled me."

"We cannot refuse this impulse any more than a salmon can ignore its instincts to return home. You must now train."

"Train? It's pitch black out here," I say, looking around.

"It will not be for long, or where you are going. The opportunity is now."

I nod, not knowing what I've gotten myself into.

He pulls up the first training module. Tanz and the campfire fade away. My body flexes and muscles tighten like a root growing stronger. I am focused. Zeroing in. Standing ready.

TRAINING

A MASTER FROM ancient Narican appears. I recognize him from the war council. He's muscular with brown eyes and a yellow third eye in his forehead that moves independently of the others. He's short with a silver flowing robe.

"My name is Syol," he says and begins pacing in a room with no windows, yellow walls. "A warrior must be strong yet flexible. We must fully know ourselves and our opponents to be victorious one hundred percent of the time. Knowing only ourselves victory will result in winning half the battles. Yet knowing ourselves and our opponent, we will win every fight.

"First, we must meditate. Connect with yourself and the energies of the universe. Eyes closed. Feel your breath and blood flow through your body. You are your thoughts. Actions stem from thought and impulse. Feel your heart pumping within your chest. Stand within your blood, connect with your cells, know your truth."

I am instantly shrunk and transported within myself. My hearts thumps and capillaries dangle, organs process. I am sucked into my heart as if a ride at the fair while on a blood flume. Swooping out of my heart into the aorta, I ride a drop of blood into blood rapids along my chest, meeting up with smaller streams. These streams create waves. I hold on tight like a canoe. *"Whoaaaa,"* I shout up to the cellular wall as I drop into my belly like a bowl, swirling around my navel and *dantian* I feel great power and see a light band of red, blue, and green, knowing that is my connection to the universe. I bounce through my hips like rapids down into the shoot of my leg. *"Ahhhhh!"* I shout, gaining speed rising up against the walls.

Past the knee and ankle, I enter my foot, knocking past small bones, horseshoe turns. The blood level lowers. Seeing the inside walls of my foot and dead end of my five toes and translucent skin. Full speed I head into the big toe like a surfer. Entering the shoot of the toe peninsula a wall of flesh stands a thousand feet high from my small cellular perspective. Bracing for impact I close my eyes, about to ram into it, *"Ahhh,"* then I'm back in my body standing in front of the master on wobbly legs. Then I fall down.

Syol continues, "When need be, your cells hold the key to all strengths and defenses. Some you will only learn when called upon."

Woozy, I nod, laying on the floor.

"We will now begin with your most natural gift, speed. Please stand."

I stumble to my feet. He moves in zigzag blurring lines. I'm seeing where he was not where he is. Though he looks as old as the moon he's faster than my eyes can follow.

"Watch with your being, eyes too slow." He taps my shoulder, standing next to me, smiles, then stands where he was at the beginning. His robe unruffled, hands in front of him at rest, eyes closed.

"You're not even breathing hard."

"Do you breathe hard when walking? Align with truth, you can move as fast as you can feel. As fast as light moves. We are Sun Clan after all."

"Impossible. I can't move as fast as light."

"The only impossibility is one's belief. The mind complicates. Do not let it. Energy is in motion, always. You cannot see that tree behind you moving, yet it vibrates with life. You must see the universe with new eyes. New understanding. Not the reality your mind conveys. Mind too slow. Quiet your mind. Allow your spiritual intelligence to see."

I close my eyes trying to clear my thoughts, not focus on any one thing, just let ideas and questions float by.

"Allow. Allow. Yes. Expand."

I open them and we are on the streets of Big City in a seedy area with rundown buildings. Four thugs surround him. Their attacks appear predictable to him. He strikes and jumps as if in slow motion. As if he knew their moves before they did. Walks through slapping them in the back of their heads. After outmaneuvering with throws, sweeps, and takedowns, he creates rings of light imprisoning all four with the slightest of motion and effort.

Wiping the scene away he moves around me like a shooting star then stops, balancing on one toe. "You shall become as I. Flawless. Perceive with your essence and all doors will open."

I nod, not exactly sure what he's talking about.

"No roadblocks, in essence."

"How do you create the rings of light? I've tried."

"I do not create rings of light. The sun does. I am but a conduit."

Placing the second foot down, he bows, and we are transported to a nebula hovering above a recently formed protostar. I grab for my throat. Can't breathe. It's sealed shut.

"You do not need to breathe." He floats, head down, eyes and mouth closed. His forehead pulsates a yellow light from his closed third eye. I hear his voice, but his mouth does not move. *"You are no longer in the third dimension and therefore the same laws do not apply."*

I try to respond, clutching my mouth, yet cannot open it. Gasping for air, trying to breathe through my nose, but my nose is also sealed. Oh no. I start to panic.

"Use your higher self," he says in my head as I pass out, falling over, floating in suspended animation.

When I come to he's in the same spot, floating. Flares of light and brilliant colors surround us.

"Telepathy is taxing for the weak in any dimension. There is no air to breathe. Use your thoughts to communicate, not your mouth."

I nod and focus really hard, close my eyes, then pass out again.

When I come to he's standing over me as a forest comes into view. I feel the hard-packed dirt under my prostrate body.

"Enough for today. Meditate on yourself and find the universe within." He bows then disappears.

I stand in the darkness of night and hear Tanz snoring from across the campsite. The campfire coals glow dimly.

In the tent my eyelids collapse with the weight of a new world opening within me.

MONSTER TRUCKS

I AWAKEN WITH the rising sun, inside the tent, getting hot. Tanz sleeps as I crawl out, zipping up the tent. Breathing deep, I fill my lungs with sweet woodland air and start to jog. I head out along the campsite loop at a warm-up pace then take it up a notch, moving faster and faster, legs thickening as my mind calms and breathing remains moderate. The loop is empty on this weekday and I observe myself, my abilities. Ten loops around, timing myself. Each loop faster. The last one was 1.2 seconds.

Back at the campsite I sit in meditation, connecting to my blood, sitting inside myself, feeling the *dantian* and cord that binds me to the universe and light gods. I feel my awareness growing. I am Claremone of the Sun Clan. I breathe deeply, listening to the air, feeling its gift of life when my eyes open once again.

Tanz stands outside the tent now. "There you are…" he says.

I stand and step closer, feeling power running through me. "Why are we here when the dark forces are growing stronger? We must fight them." I do a few strikes and kicks in front of him.

He smirks. "We're buying time and keeping you safe. Clearly the fresh air has done you good." He smiles, walks over to the picnic table, grabs a broccoli crown, and gnaws on it.

"There is more I must tell you. Sit."

I breathe in my essence and sit upon a log.

"There is one thing and one thing only in the human's favor: the soul. An incorruptible soul is placed inside every sentient being. In a very real sense the soul is a beacon of truth to one's larger self. It is similar in design to that of a lighthouse creating a lit path to port bringing in a ship during a storm. No matter how confused or clouded a mind becomes that beacon can always bring them home."

"Like Narican is to the dimensions?"

He nods. "That is a wise observation." He pulls up the equation and sprinkles this in. "77% Complete." It calculates then is wiped away.

A pick-up truck rumbles into the campground kicking up gravel and dirt. Rifles hang from the rear window as the truck skids to a laughing stop three campsites over. Music blasts from open windows though the morning is still early. Beer cans fall out when doors crack open.

"Hunters." Alarmed, Tanz stands, studying them, stepping closer. "We must leave," he says and turns to pack up food on the picnic table.

"Why? They're just hunters."

He looks at me. "Have you learned nothing? If they see my eyes they may become startled and shoot. They are easy prey for dark force scouts."

We pack up the food, roll the tent and sleeping bags, and squeeze them into the motorcycle cases. The key is turned and the 1200 cc engine comes alive. Startled, the hunters look over. Tanz throttles it as a smirk grows on his face. We nod to each other, hop on, rolling out the opposite way of the loop heading onto State Road north.

Opening the gears, Tanz hits a hundred and ten in the early morning air, with no cars around, blues skies and rusty sun overhead. I have a crazy idea and stand up on the foot pegs.

"Whooo hoo!" I shout, when an idea comes to me.

"Can I run this fast?"

I think about it. Hmm, could die.

Then I jump off the bike with legs pumping. My feet catch the ground. The bike moves like it's taking a leisurely jog around the block. Tanz looks over and revs it out, dropping it into the next gear, and pulls ahead. I move a little quicker and pass him. After a few seconds I spring back on. Tanz gives me a thumbs up as we roar off on the bike.

After another hour riding, we see signs for Jebadon Motor Speedway. He points to the sign throttling the motorcycle engine faster. It screams, approaching the red line, and the speedometer bounces at 137.

The vast parking lot is empty. We ride to the far side of the track and ditch the bike in a bush. Peeking over the racing wall a slew of hot rods and race cars sit dormant.

His blue eyes grow wide as we jump over the wall. At a jog we pass the cars.

Looking back, I ask, "Aren't we stopping?"

He shakes his head past the souped-up sports cars with wing-like spoilers. Past a large metal building I now see where we're going as monster trucks come into sight lined up like giant steel beasts, resting in silence, because no one has yet woken them up. Our pace slows as we approach the six trucks.

"You knew these trucks were here?" I ask.

He nods, smiling, inspecting each one.

"I thought you didn't watch monster trucks?"

"I never said anything of the sort."

I stare back at the race cars. My longing to drive one is dashed.

With blue waves, he pulls up diagnostics of the truck Bucking Bronco.

"Oh, I enjoyed watching them very much," he says, climbing aboard and strapping himself in with the door open at my eye level.

"Get in."

"Are you sure this is a necessary means, Tanz?"

"Oh yes. Quite necessary."

The engine fires up like an explosion coming alive. This feels like a bad idea. I climb up the other side and strap in. He nods, staring straight ahead, muscling it into gear.

We bounce along slowly in first gear then out into the open arena of the speedway. Tanz runs out the engine, popping it into second gear then third. The truck lurches forward, growling louder, bouncing. We move past the cars. At the far end of the track is a jump field. He seems to be aiming for that, dropping it into fourth gear. We bounce and jostle and pick up speed. I hold on for dear life. He pumps the accelerator, pegging it to the floor.

"Hold on."

Bracing against the dash I ask, "What are you doing?" I say, studying the jump, wall, and fast approaching trees. Ascending the ramp full speed. Lifting off my stomach drops as we soar high over the speedway wall then slam down onto the hard earth in the heavy machine. We bounce and sway on the shocks. I'm terrified while a smile is glued to his face.

"I didn't realize Earth could be so pleasing," he says, ramming it into low gear as we bounce up the hillside through brush to tucked-away power lines.

We trounce and bounce and eat up the trail, blowing by a dog walker. After a few miles of whip lashing bumps, the power lines come to an end, and nestled houses disappear. We roll through bushes that scrape the doors and undercarriage of the truck like fingernails on a chalkboard.

A swamp rests ahead within a deep watery forest. Muck flies off the giant paddlewheel like tires as we enter the vast swamp, leaving solid earth behind along with my stomach. I don't like the eerie feeling and growing fear of getting stuck dying in the mud.

Tanz studies the terrain. The mud sucks to the truck tires like an octopus. The windows are half-caked.

I swear I just saw an alligator then another scrambling behind a bush. We continue at a slow pace. Up ahead rests a grassy rise and swamp's end. I swallow and lean forward. A pool of shallow water holds about fifty gators who fight, hunt, and bathe. They snap as the truck passes slowly by. My heart stops. Don't let them puncture a tire. Don't let them puncture a tire, I pray. "Are you sure you know what you're doing?"

Tanz white knuckles the steering wheel.

"Uh, huh," is all he mutters, staring out the windshield.

Powering up the hill we bounce onto hard land and find a ramshackle barn leaning on stilts a few hundred yards up. It sits over the stream that feeds the swamp. Parking the truck half leaning on a small red maple tree that's ready to snap, he jumps out, smiling. "I'm famished." He claps his hands together.

I sit unmoving, dazed, in the truck, my head still bouncing. From behind his seat he grabs the food and hard cases. Paranoid, I step slowly down from the cab making certain no gators are underfoot.

Once I'm on the grass I pause, looking around. "This has nothing to do with your cooking but, *blxxkk*." I stoop over, puking.

"Last one in the barn is a rotting egg," he says, striding up the barn ramp.

"That's rotten, egg. *Bllkkkxx*," I say, puking again.

BARN

SITTING ON THE rotting floorboards in a one room barn, I wonder as I'm setting up for the night, if the stream below is wide enough for gators. I don't ask. I hear splashing below and try to focus on eating my turkey and broccoli as the dark night creeps closer. I can't stop my mind from running away with these scary thoughts.

"I think the dark forces have me, Tanz."

"Why's that?"

"I'm scared of alligators."

He laughs. "It's natural to fear alligators. Now get some rest."

I keep thinking the gators are coming up from the swamp, smelling us. Maybe they live in the barn too. The sun has gone down and so has my last hope of protection. I feel like a child again, afraid of the dark.

After dinner I drift off in the creaking barn. Hearing the grunting and hissing sounds of the gators. I dream of dark forces floating in their hypnotic black eyes marching toward us as we sleep.

Startled awake. "Tanz. Tanz, are you awake?" I ask, sitting up.

"I find myself to be now."

"I can't sleep."

"Shall we work?" he inquires.

"Yes. Please. I need to think about something else."

I hear him shift and a sliver of moonlight catches his laser blue eyes. "I was going to wait until morning but since we're awake and the dark forces are certainly awake, we best get to work. We are partially blind to their intentions, yes?" He brings up his incomplete blue pulsating equation that hangs in the air, illuminating the room like a nightlight, waiting for the right components to be entered.

"We don't know who's behind this. So let's begin with what we do know." He places each bit of information into the blue light equation. It's instantly absorbed. "When did you turn eighteen?"

"Less than a week ago…"

"And when did these changes begin?"

"Less than a week ago…"

"They've been watching you… waiting…"

"I feel like my whole life people have been watching me. Teachers in school, parents would look at me in weird ways."

"They have. I'm sorry."

"Was anything real? Even my nasty relatives at holiday parties?"

"Well, that was your drunk uncle who pushed your father once. Awkwardness, meanness, cruel judgments are not necessarily the dark forces at work but one's own conflicted conscience. That's why Earth is a battleground. Good has not prevailed over evil. And equations without all their pieces are unsolvable riddles."

He adds and rearranges segments and they light up, taking shape. "All images past and present are alive. The universe does not know death or time. That's why memories are often more alive now than they were when they first happened. Their clarity has grown. The moment is isolated." He looks at the Akashich records again and shakes his head. "It is not there yet must be."

"Perhaps they encoded or filed it incorrectly on purpose?"

"Impossible. Accounting is about known factors, not conjecture. Let's get back to the list. Known factors often lead to unknown and soon to be known factors."

"Like following breadcrumbs," I say.

He nods. "Surrogate family, dead. No siblings." He lists this information like, well, an accountant would. "Dreams of Narican?" I nod. He sprinkles it in.

"No powers so far but speed. Has begun the transformation and alignment process. Has begun the training in connective meditation, levitation, ESP, war rings, and is growing stronger daily. Eats a healthy diet of turkey and broccoli. Dark forces are growing exponentially. Job infiltrated and is wanted dead."

"Yup, let's not forget that," I say.

"We are now on the lam figuring out our next move. Gaining strength. Reconnecting DNA. Taking Iron Core Crystals."

"Oh, and that you can hotwire stuff…" I say chiming in.

He ignores me and stands, analyzing the haze cluster that attempted to rob the old man. He saved me while they gnawed on me. I can still feel the pain in my ribs.

"There are no permanent cells to scan. Haze forms are too scattered. There's no substance within a single intent of aggression, confusion, or befuddlement. No root cells, no memories, only murky impulses. Their histories are as murky and obfuscated as their gaseous bodies. We must do better. Narican has already grown dark. The rest of the universe could fall: a moonless night for the gods to be sure.

"The records were created as a historical database, not to find criminals. I can only access histories. I cannot scan everything. That would take lifetimes. You must help me, Claremone." His eyes intensify and hypnotize me. I look away.

"How?" I ask.

"I cannot scan your life. One picture alone has a million bits of information. I must get closer to the source. You must remember events that stand out."

"I'm sorry. I don't know anything."

We fall silent with the gators nearby. I try to focus. An owl flies off a rafter above and out a glassless window. *"Hooo. Hooo."* It scares me three quarters to death. Water splashes and the swamp sounds close in. I try meditating on events and clear my head but the boards creak under me as I shift, trying to think.

"Wait, a woman came into the shop and touched my arm. And that tattooed guy came and saw you on line."

"Their cells will remember." Tanz walks over and places his hands on me. The boards creak and bend even more as our weight sinks in place.

He speaks in measured monotones as blue images play. "They entered your energy field. They received orders… to test you… study you…That is why she touched your arm and he was rude. They were to test you and report back."

"To who?" I ask. "Testing me, what did she see?"

"They were planning to ambush you and take your life…" Tanz plays the image and intention placed in them to kill me in an alley. Watching, I can feel the lifeforce ripped out.

"That's comforting," I say, looking away. "She had orders? Who's her boss?" I'm getting pissed off now, wanting payback. I'm still alive and will keep being so. Equations jump through the air erasing and rewriting. He calculates, tracking DNA imprints where she spends most of her time.

He tracks space and time to a warehouse in the textile district and the image of a low-level pain dealer who sells dark forces on the open market. The man is scruffy with a strange bump on his head.

On the brick building advertisements read, "Will ruin any relationship $500; car steering failure $750; broken bones $1000; any death $5000 and receive a free trip to the Bahamas!" Haze and dark forces surround the building.

"Looks like a real winner," I say.

Tanz sits down. "It's worse than I thought. Upon our return, we must be careful."

"Careful? Now we're returning?"

"Yes, we will need you as bait."

"Bait? Don't they want me dead? Didn't you see that image?" I swallow hard, stomping around, forgetting about the damn creaking boards.

"Yes. That's why you're the bait. Makes perfect sense, no? We must find this dark force dealer, Qualmsy."

"Qualmsy?"

"Yes, Qualmsy is his name." Tanz lies back down to rest, satisfied with our progress. The equation waves in blue over him after he sprinkles in this information.

"82% Complete." He rolls over and says, "Sweet dreams."

"This is not going to help me sleep, Tanz." I'm not sure which is worse, gators or people wanting to kill me. I lay down on the sleeping bag with a racing mind.

Tossing and turning, sitting up and laying down, I can feel the bending in the boards soft from years sitting over the creak.

Restless, I sit up and lie down once more trying to get comfortable when the boards break. I fall five feet into the cold rushing water. Startled, now in the muddy water, the air is black and impenetrable. I see nothing but shadows of moonlight. Hissing and grunting scurry toward me. Black eyes from the bushes creep forward.

Tanz jumps down. His eyes glow like flashlights but the beasts don't slow their approach. Out from the bushes the hissing and grunting grow louder.

There must be ten of them with immense slick and ridged bodies. I hear Tanz inhale deeply then let out a sound that can only be described as half-donkey, half-wolf.

"Hyyyrrrooo!"

Unleashing this terrible call works. The gators scurry back into the bushes. He yanks me into the barn and tells me to stay close to the wall. "Joists are stronger there."

Shivering, shaking, wet and muddy, I change and crawl into the sleeping bag. "What was that awful noise you made scaring half the swamp?"

"Oh, that? That was a bloomdiphous. A two headed beast from Narican that puts fear into its prey. I learned the call when I was a boy. Even won some competitions."

"Oh, I see… Well you saved my life again. I owe you. Thanks," I say, warming up and closing my eyes now somehow calmer.

Drifting off, I hear him say, "You will have your opportunities."

RETURNING TO THE CITY

THE NEXT DAY we ditch the truck in a sea of juniper bushes. At least it's not a swamp. We jump down from the truck cab. The poor thing has nearly broken down, Tanz beat on it so hard. Smoke pours out of the hood. We walk the last few miles to the city from the outlying woods. Hacking through bushes I ask, "Do you even have a license?"

"For what?" he responds without a hint of sarcasm.

I shake my head laughing.

The last half mile are prickers, muck, trash, and mosquitoes.

"Why again are we going back?" I ask, seeing the cityscape down below.

"We are Sun Clan and it is our duty. That does not change with risk."

"So we're soldiers?"

"Of sorts. We essentially work for the gods."

"Soldier gods?"

"Not quite. The Sun Clan DNA within our cells was placed there by the gods as protectors. We are their last line of defense."

"Well, what's the first?"

"The people themselves of course."

"So, we're going back to warn them?"

He stops walking. "People will be frightened if we speak the truth. Truth frightens them." He grows thoughtful. "Their minds will shut down and they will become violent. History has proven that humans become aggressive when a new idea is shown to them. It challenges their way of being. The new and unknown scares them. It is out of the norm thus violence ensues. We must find this Qualmsy ourselves and deal with him," he says, and takes up moving again.

We make it to the tip of the city and inconspicuously stroll along Century Boulevard. I'm happy to be on concrete again. Within the first block we see haze balls floating and shifting in front of stores like drug dealers. There are more than when we left. They grab people coming out of stores with beers and cigarettes, recruiting it seems, as they envelope them. I avert my eyes.

People walk through and their dispositions change.

Two blocks down, Tanz spots a middle-aged woman crying with a tissue to her nose sitting on a sidewalk bench on the other side of the road. "Stop." He puts his hands up, watching this colorful being hover over the woman.

"Come," he says and begins crossing the street.

"I thought we were staying hidden."

"We must gather information when it presents itself." He stops in the middle of the street. Cars honk. "We are all that's left, Claremone. Do you understand what this means? If we fail, darkness spreads, devouring all that is light." He continues walking. Several drivers flip him the bird, which he ignores then says, "Concerned citizens," stepping onto the curb.

I stand, confused, now several feet behind him up on the sidewalk. "But isn't that a dark force? What are you doing?"

"You are wrong. There are others."

SPIRIT ANGEL

WE GET CLOSER and this floating creature is a woman with flowing sapphire hair imbued with golden highlights. Rainbow colors undulate through her like waves through water. Light permeates. She floats, smiling, enveloping this crying woman as if comforting her. The woman on the bench seems kind with soft eyes and a warmth beneath her sorrow.

I've never sensed such compassion before. We stand within a few feet now. The spirit smiles at the woman, glowing with radiant love without words, while floating above her.

"That's what I thought," Tanz whispers to me. "There is a veil between this world and the Homdin. Humans cannot see these spirits other than out of the corner of their eye as a trick of the light."

"Ho… Hom… what?"

He leans over and whispers, "This colorful woman is not a dark force but a spirit guide hovering and comforting."

"Who is she?"

"Not who, what. Spirit guides watch over this planet yet cannot be revealed."

In awe, we watch longer. Her aura glows with the pure intention of love. My body tingles and I feel like a baby in the arms of my mother. I don't want to leave or move but lay down on the sidewalk to nap.

"They are evolved beings that gather in the outer reaches of Earth's atmosphere. They choose to stay here on this planet and give comfort." He pulls my arm and we walk a few feet away so as not to disturb her.

"They are pure energy and intention yet speak no words."

"So, in basic terms she's like a dark force, but a good force?"

"To overly simplify, yes. The intention of one's energy creates the colors of one's aura or energy field. You're looking dazed at me again."

"I'm eighteen, remember? This is all a little beyond me."

Tanz shakes his head. "They're friends yet live by a different set of universal laws."

"I didn't know the universe was so complicated."

He furrows his brow and I think rolls his eyes. "You sure you didn't…?

"Yes, yes, I must've bumped my head. I know."

The woman guide hovers over this grieving woman. Her aura shimmers. Colored lights dance through her body like sunlight through stained glass. Her eyes glow soft and warm.

Tanz grabs my arm, we step closer again. He warns, "We must be cautious; we cannot interrupt her directive from God."

"God?" I swallow.

Tanz nods. "The head of spirits is named God. That's his name. Spirit God, God of Spirits, Leader. They are a collective. He is their being head and they work from the same impulse as a school of fish. Nature is governed by these electrical impulses that maintain symbiosis. You sure you weren't hit on the head?"

"Why do people keep asking me this? I'm eighteen, man, and have pimples. Someone tried to kill me a couple days ago and it seems throughout my entire life!"

"Right, so pay attention."

I shake my head as we get closer and Tanz moves to speak with the spirit lady. She's surprised and looks up. My guess is no one has ever spoken to her before in this dimension. His forehead pulsates with light. She smiles gently, nodding. He leans into her energy field and the light of it. Peace comes over his face. "Delightful," is all he says. His body is next to mine but clearly he is elsewhere.

He leans back out, touching his heart, and nods. "Thank you," he says to her in a whisper.

She nods, returning to the mourning woman.

Walking away in silence, my heart is happy and full. After another minute and down another block, Tanz says, "She doesn't understand the increased suffering in the world or know where the dark forces are coming from. She is only certain of love."

After another block, Tanz stops. "We must get to the apartments. There are a few things I need. Go to yours and get anything you can't live without. Then meet me at the Botanical Gardens downtown."

"In all this you want to look at flowers?"

"Angry people do not seek out flowers," he says, and walks off.

Over his shoulder I hear, "Meet me in one hour. Speak to no one… look at no one… eyes reveal truth."

I nod and take one step then stop. "But what about your equations on the walls?"

He stops and turns to me, now standing a few feet away. "They live within me. We must find this Qualmsy and deal with his underground network that sells pain and destruction. Speak to no one, and if you see something do not stop." He steps away then stops again. "There is something unstable about that boy Dino and his sister. You are weak to them. Stay away." This gives me the chills.

Upon parting I realize the warmth of the day is baking my shirt and burning my face.

*

Something's wrong in my apartment. I step in and quickly notice the fire escape window is up. The walls have graffiti on them in red paint. My bed is cut up and tossed. Pillow feathers lay on the floor. My desk is knocked over and broken. My laptop gone. A strange symbol is drawn on the wall. I step closer. It matches the tattoo on that guy's face. I check the apartment making certain no one is hiding to assault me. After what Tanz told me with them wanting to kill me, I can't be too cautious. I check every door and crevice. Nothing.

Back into the living room I step past rubble into the middle and see some weird medieval séance on the floor. A trail of blood or something red outlines the perimeter of the room to an ashed-over fire that must've been only inches in size. I bend, seeing a half-burned picture of me. A picture I've never seen but one taken while working at the store. It was from outside on the sidewalk.

I study it and stand, feeling as if I'm being watched again, as if I'm the one on trial.

I throw the picture down. "I'm right here, damn it!" I say, spinning in all directions. "Enough with these games. Come get me if you want me."

A panel of robed, faceless judges shimmer, making no move, but watch from beyond the horizon, waiting, observing.

Oh, no, the picture of my parents is smashed. I hurry over and pick it up, cradling it for a second.

"I'm so sorry. This is all my fault," I say to them, removing the picture from the broken frame. I fold it and place it into my back pocket. Moving broken drawers out of my way I look under the desk. My drawings of Narican are gone. I stand and sigh, dropping my shoulders. Along the wall under my bed I find the *Tao Te Ching*, grab that, stuff some clothes and books into the backpack.

Stepping to the door, I want to stop at Other Worlds to see Caesar. He always helps with advice and is a friendly face, but I don't have time. Tanz said to keep moving.

I look around the apartment. "They can have it," I say and slam the door on my way out.

Wondering what happened, the fire and burned picture disturb me. Pensively down the stairs I step into the rusty sunlight again.

The hard sidewalk and noise zoom around me like a beehive. After a few paces I see Dino and his sister half a block up petting a small brown dog. They do always seem to be around when I am. About to turn the other way Dino sees me and runs over.

"Reuben!" he shouts.

Laurie-Ann jogs up behind him. "There you are," she says with a smile on her face.

I can't stop him from hugging me.

"I thought you went on a trip," she says with confusion on her face.

I hear Tanz in my head telling me to keep away.

"Yeah, I was… I am. Plus, I just got robbed." I look up at the building.

"Oh, no. What did they take?" she says.

Shaking my head, not sure if I can trust her, I say stepping away, "I'm sorry, I have to go."

"You know, you were kind of a jerk last time. Like you're being now. What, you can't talk to us anymore?"

One pace away I stop and turn. "No, it's not that. Just some heavy stuff going on I can't explain."

"I'll say. Come on, Dino." She grabs his hand and drags her brother away.

"Bye, Reuben," he says, waving, her back to me.

"Bye, buddy."

Tanz is right. I am weak to them.

GRAND BOTANICAL GARDENS

HE'S WAITING OUTSIDE the gates when I arrive. Tanz stares at me and says, "Things have gotten worse." He's bleeding from the lip and seems frail like an old man.

"Are you okay? My place was vandalized."

"Shh, wait until we get inside." Tanz pays the admission with exact change. The ticket booth woman gives us sideways glances. Smaller city buildings stand close by.

Inside the wrought iron gate, we pass a cluster of apple trees.

Tanz says, "I smelled sulfur then someone knocked me down."

Among rose bushes a hundred yards in we find a bench down a small path covered with wood chips. He sits scanning himself with imagery stopping at a floating haze ball around the corner in his apartment. Then a punch comes from the side. Turning the image, he tracks the arm back to the man with the symbol under his eye, the same guy in the grocery store, and probably the one in my apartment.

Tanz falls to the floor and the scruffy man kicks him. Tanz passes out.

"Weirdo," is all the man says. The recording continues.

Staring at equations all over the apartment the thug says, "What the...?" Peeking in front and behind walls he rubs his chin. He tries grabbing the images, but his hands pass through. In confusion he kicks Tanz again.

Tanz's nose drips blood as he slumps forward on the green bench.

"Can you go on? Do you need a hospital? You look awful," I say, placing my hand on his shoulder.

"I am bound by blood to continue."

"An accountant soldier, huh? Bad ass." I nod approvingly and try making him laugh. "I once heard, 'Pride takes a hit the same time as one's face...' "

"Yes, I too have heard this, and my case appears to confirm that." He smiles with a wry grin. "However, emotions have never clouded mathematical equations."

"So, what's the plan, Tanzy?"

"My name," he says, sitting up with eyes glowing, "is Tanz. Two blocks from here lies Qualmsy and his network. We begin there. That is the plan. First, we store our things here behind these rose bushes. The bushes should mask any scent." He stands while his words grow more confident.

"There is a safe house, an abandoned church on Miranda and Ostrand. If we get separated meet there, second floor rear. Now let us find this Qualmsy who will surely lead us up the chain. For if there is a chain, there is always a chain-maker..."

THE PAIN DEALER

AT THE TAIL end of rush hour people come and go. Perfect for us to blend in as we peek around the corner at the building one block away.

Tanz lectures me. "A hornet's nest awaits. So, stay calm. Anger begets anger. Aggression begets aggression. We cannot go in fighting. We will lose."

I nod, ready to spin fists and feet.

A haze envelopes the building top as a rain cloud would. My arm hairs bristle as I cross the street. It's colder here, clammy.

The tattoo guy with the symbol under his eye stands out front with four other goons looking mean.

"What do you want?" Tattoo says like any tough guy would stepping down to me.

I put on my best outlaw voice and say, "Payback for what you did."

The goons tighten in, ready for a fight, sleeves rolling up. I study them squinting my eyes like Clint Eastwood would, then release. "Nah, just kidding. I'm here to see Qualmsy with a deal."

Tattoo pokes me in the chest. "That's *Mister* Qualmsy to you. But wait, how do you know who our boss is? That might not be his name," he says, crossing his arms and nodding to an associate who follows suit.

Oh boy, these guys are dumb.

Tattoo raises a fist to strike me when his associate whispers into his ear.

"I know, I know." He shrugs the buffoon off and types something into his watch. The door pops open behind them.

Tattoo and Beefcake #2 escort me down a freight elevator. The other three remain in front.

"So, you're some kind of freak, huh?" Tattoo asks, staring at me once the door closes.

"Nope, just a regular guy." I look straight ahead without making eye contact.

"I hear ya," he says, bopping his head. "Yup, me too."

I look but there are no floor numbers, so I count seconds in my head. Seven seconds pass then the doors open to a palatial room with red carpet and red velvet curtains. Haze balls rush up and swirl around my head. They smell horrible, like rotting garbage and sulfur. A whistle calls them off from the far side of the room. Qualmsy, I presume.

Businessmen along the walls are being beaten. Haze balls exact pain, ecstasy. Some men weep on the floor. "Oh, this is horrible. Give me more." More haze balls encircle him. "Oh, yeah. Oh, yeah. That's it," he says.

Another man shouts, "I'm bad. I'm so bad. I was mean to my wife…" He weeps on a chair.

I'm shoved farther into the room. Qualmsy and others sit on plush sofas. The woman who pulled my arm at the grocery store sits a few feet away from him. Others play cards.

Haze balls float above Qualmsy, some rest nearby upon rafters, armchairs, some roll around together on the floor like cats playing.

TV monitors line a side wall. Displays of muggings on street corners and in stores, thefts, people drinking too much, fighting in the streets. There's war, explosions, more war, protests, and violence.

I step closer and now see what the extra skin on Qualmsy's forehead is—an extra nose just beneath his hairline.

Tanz had warned me: that somehow he's developed this to smell sulfur nearby and control it. Smaller haze balls rest within his black curly hair like a nest. He strokes them gently as a father would.

"Don't you love the smell of sulfur on a rainy day?" It seems like a rhetorical question that I don't answer. He grabs a haze ball floating nearby and rubs his face in it, breathing deeply. "Ahh." He releases the ball and it floats off giggling.

Accepting what my eyes see, I try to sound strong like Tanz and I had discussed.

I step forward. "Since you've been looking for me, I figured I'd save you the trouble. You know, you and I aren't so different. Maybe we could work out a deal. I'll work with you, but not for you. With my abilities what are you willing to pay? Or perhaps I could buy my claim back. What was their offer?" I step closer still.

He puts up his hand. "Stop. You don't have that kind of money, boy. I saw where you worked and lived."

Speechless, he'd seen my apartment. "So, you and Tattoo broke into my place. Why?"

He studies me. "I'm simply a businessman hired for a service."

"Again, what are my services worth to you?" I say more bluntly. Tired of this game. Tired of my whole life being a game. "Your boss, Mister… I forget his name… would pay an awful lot…"

"I would consider a deal if you had anything I needed. Besides, we know your friend, the Accountant, *ooohhh,*" he says, shaking his hands as laughter fills the room, "is waiting outside." He types into his watch.

One monitor switches to Tanz getting beat up in an alley.

"No!" I lunge at Qualmsy, but the thugs stop me.

"Bring him in," he speaks into his watch. "We've been looking for him, too. And now we have you both. You made it so much easier on me. I thank you."

They bring Tanz in and throw him to the floor in front of Qualmsy. Beefcake #3 lifts him up, punches him in the face and stomach, and drops him to the floor again. Tanz chokes, coughing up blood.

"Enough." Qualmsy stands. "Our client has plans for these two. An old man and a weak boy. Scary stuff." He spreads out his arms and shouts, "Is this the toughest this town has to offer? Give me a break." He lowers his head and stares at us.

Tanz flashes his eyes and blue waves radiate, but Qualmsy laughs. "No, no, no, sir. Save your strength," he says, waving his hand as if brushing it aside. The woman cowers on the sofa. Qualmsy offers her solace. "It's all right, my dear. He cannot harm you."

"Thank you, Mr. Qualmsy." She speaks meekly. His confidence relaxes her; her face turns mean again.

"What kind of grandfather brings a boy to a place like this, anyway?"

They stand me up and punch me in the stomach, dropping me to the floor next to Tanz. I can't breathe. Fire crashes into my brain, eyes watering. My solar plexus spasms, grasping for air.

Tattoo says, "I've been waitin' to do that."

Qualmsy steps closer. "You two are having a really bad day, hmm? Well, it's gonna get worse."

"You'll pay for that," I say.

"No, I've already *been* paid for that." He chuckles, turning to watch the monitors. "Must see TV, gentlemen."

"We're connected," I say.

He turns quickly. "That's not what I heard. Besides, I have an army. And what does your store sell, granola and milk? Are you going to beat me with a protein bar and blue chips?" He shakes his head. "Quite a fearsome duo."

Laughter fills the room again from ghastly faces and corrupt humans. Even the businessmen on the side laugh.

"Why have you been tracking us anyway?" I ask.

"I know everything about you, boy. Even your dead parents. So sad. Terrible accident."

I get quiet and ask, "You did that?"

"Think of me as a caring uncle who's watched you grow. Now that I think of it, I could use an errand boy, and well, Slim, you could do my taxes." They all laugh again. "This is just too comical." He slaps his knee, strolling to the sofa. "I can't get enough of these two."

Rage grows inside me and my legs begin twitching. Blood boiling. I can taste revenge.

Tanz covers his pulsating forehead. *"No, Claremone. Not yet. Channel this anger."*

I calm, growing faint.

"You should be a standup comedian, Mr. Qualmsy." The woman says then cowers as he stares disapprovingly at her.

He grabs another floating haze ball and inhales it using both noses. This time he throws it to the floor.

Tanz speaks in my head again. *"We are not strong enough to defeat them. Wait for the right opportunity. One will present itself."* Then his arms give out on the floor and he passes out.

I grow dizzy from the telepathy, can't see straight and fall to my knees. "Please, sir, we offer our services." One last attempt knowing we have to get out of here.

"Boy, what you offer I have never needed. I'm a businessman and you are simply out of business. We've waited for years to kill you. Don't take that away from us." He steps closer and shouts, "Take them to the Rack!" His hands flail violently, and the goons grab us.

Tattoo jams his elbow into my ribs. "I really like doing that to you."

Leaning on Beefcake #3 Tanz tries to touch Qualmsy by falling forward with extended hands but the bruiser blocks him.

Qualmsy steps off, bending down to meet his gaze. "I know your game, Slim. I don't know how, but you won't be reading me. I've been warned about you: some kind of psychic mind reader. Gives me the heebie jeebies." He stands and grabs another haze ball.

We're turned to be escorted out. The wall behind us has a dozen hanging shirts with live faces trapped inside them.

Qualmsy shouts. "Our client doesn't even want his free trip to the Bahamas!"

Then after a pause, he shouts again, "Wait! Stop! Make printed shirts out of them, so I can hang them on the wall with my other souvenirs. Then we'll deliver the goods."

*

The Rack is a room with an old clothes rack for hanging and stretching material connected to a metal production line that runs along a steel track above.

A glass wall rests with an immense gray machine on the other side that feeds the rack. Sprayers for dye and a steaming vat of boiling water bubbles in front. Plain white shirts hang at the end awaiting imprint and ink.

Once we step into the room, they spritz us with something that makes my head go foggy. My legs weaken. They spritz Tanz and his legs give out.

They punch me in the gut, and I go down. Shaking my head trying to see straight as a kick comes into my ribs.

"The toxins," says Tanz weakly, breathing hard, eyes watering then he endures another blow.

"Now, Claremone, now." On all fours his words slur like a disoriented bull after a sword slashed him.

I try moving my legs but can only straighten them, feeling weak. My body slackens. Listing from side to side, Tanz drops to the floor, eyes closing.

My vision and thoughts disorient. I'm seeing double. Beefcake Brothers move to the door standing like unblinking beasts.

Beefcake #4 must be three hundred pounds and six-five. He picks me up like a feather with one hand while Tanz lays in a heap.

He clamps my hands into the metal clothesline with heavy steel clips. *Ahhh. It hurts so bad.* Metal pierces the skin, digging in. The pain travels up my arm as metal nubs cut in around the knuckles. Tanz wakes, letting out a howl of pain as the clips sink into his flesh. We dangle several feet above the concrete floor.

My sight returns slightly. I pulse my body trying to wake it up. Behind the window, Tattoo adjusts knobs and switches. The rack bounces alive with a groaning rumble and rolls upon metal wheels to the boiling water and dye. Tanz will be first. My hands ache from the metal nubs cutting in. I try making a fist, but my hands throb too much.

Four television monitors with abuses hang to entertain as we move to the vat and suffering, to remain permanently trapped inside a shirt.

On one monitor, an old woman is mugged and her purse stolen. I look closer and it's the same old lady I helped that first day. The greasy mugger grabs her purse and pushes her to the ground. No one is there to help her.

I'm angry. Sick of all this crap, all these spreading lies and abuses. People deserve better. I want to knock the dark forces back to where they came from. Impulses tear at me from within. My brain fires, legs twitch. Flex and release. Flex and release.

In a dull, disinterested cadence Beefcake #4 says, "The water boils off the body and the toxins remove the essence. Then the colorful dyes make a beautiful shirt." He begins humming some happy tune, turning from us to check levels with a stick. His dull eyes look up again from a few feet away as we bounce closer. "It is a very interesting process." He's humming something that sounds like a nursery rhyme or a song sang at camp.

"We have to get out of here," Tanz mutters, eyes half open, studying the room.

Clear vision has returned. Only two thugs stand at the door now. Tattoo is in the room on the other side of the glass. Only Beefcake #4 is close.

Tanz calls him over. "Excuse me, young man?"

Beefcake #4 steps closer, holding the measuring stick. "Yes, sir, how may I help you?" Blue waves float out from Tanz's eyes.

Black soulless eyes stare back. "Old man, I have no fear or remorse. They have been cut away from my emotions. I am quite sorry. You will make a fine shirt," he says, going back to his humming, now bopping his head from right to left.

Tanz and I are confused. His hands are bleeding. I need to get him out of here and fast. That attempt was clearly everything he had, his eyes close again as we descend toward the vat. The machine groans. Five feet, four feet, three feet, two.

Beefcake #4 releases what must be the toxins from a tub with strange writing. Blue and green inks spray as we descend.

Willing my legs to move, aligning with my cells, my legs rotate once, twice, then stop. I flex and release, flex and release, pumping my blood, wiggling my toes and feet, willing my heart to work harder. I do it again, closing my eyes and concentrating all energies as if trying to jumpstart a car while thinking about the sun's power.

A fire burns inside and my legs stutter, pumping, then stutter again like a rusty, seized up machine. Tanz's feet dangle in the steam as we drop lower. Slowly my legs raise up and down, up and down, like jogging in place, up and down, up and down. I'm catching fire now.

The thugs don't hear the revving sound over the groaning machine. My thickening legs create friction and heat, like thick steel pistons pumping. I am moving up and down, up and down.

The movement catches Beefcake #4's eyes.

He stands, hand on hip, and asks, "Sir, who are you?"

"Well, who are you?" I ask in return, feeling the power of the Sun Clan growing in my bones.

He steps closer, wagging his finger at me. "No, no, no, sir," he says.

I pop him in the head and chest knocking him halfway across the room.

The other two beefcakes rush me. I flip up, releasing my hands and pop them so hard with my spinning pinwheel legs and hands they fly off into the air like nothing even touched me. They get wedged into the plaster wall.

Inches from the boiling water and swirling toxins I jump up, releasing Tanz then kick the rack, snapping it in two.

Surprised by my ability, I say to Tanz as we stand alone for the moment, "I didn't know I could do that. I've only run fast before. This time my hands moved equally fast." I hold out my powerful, rock-hard fists.

"Aligning with Source you are. The iron crystals in your blood have mixed with your cells, unfolding them."

Alarms sound and Qualmsy's voice comes over a speaker: "All security to the Rack. That old man and little boy cannot leave here. One free trip to the Bahamas for whoever gets 'em!"

I consider the door but that seems like a bad idea.

"What do we do?" I turn in all directions, seeking escape.

"Can you go up?" asks Tanz.

I look at the plaster above. "There's a ceiling, Tanz."

"Yes, and we're below ground. Through doors will not help."

I do see his point.

Tattoo rushes me from the machine room. I sidestep and hurl him twenty feet, feeling flawless, powerful.

The metal door flies open. Several more deadened eyes stare in.

"I'll try. But it'll be a short ride if it doesn't work." I grab Tanz. My legs pump and rotate. My body thickens like a battering ram. The deafening sound increases, wind blows the hanging shirts. My skin tightens, eyes close. We lift off the floor, hovering as they lunge at us. I cover Tanz then smash up through the ceiling.

Sounds of snapping wood and flooring, the taste of plaster dust on my lips. Up through another floor and ceiling, past two young girls playing cards on the floor nearby, then through another floor and ceiling breaking through to crash land on the roof under a dark sky of haze clusters. Plaster dust is all over us like ghosts. We tumble and roll. Tanz rolls off the edge. I grab his wrist quickly and yank him up.

The haze and dark forces that float around the building descend with scary, agonized faces. Entities *are* trapped inside them. I can see and hear them moaning with anger, in pain.

"Don't look at them," he says. "They will disorient you. And I am not strong enough."

The roof door is kicked open and several beefy guys spread out carrying bats, crowbars, knives. The dark forces move in, attempting to gnaw on us. I shrug one off my shoulder but three more come. I swat them away as I rotate around Tanz, protecting him. Eyeballing the building across the street.

Tanz shakes his head. "You cannot make it. We must find an alternative escape. What you just did should have drained you."

"No, I feel good. I can make it," I say, eyeballing the next roof. More dark forces float up through heat ducts and roof vents.

My legs have stopped for the moment only because I put the brakes on, having learned to control them. As the dark cloud closes in, I feel sorrow, anguish, heartache.

"We have no choice." I start my legs up again grabbing Tanz.

"You're going to kill us," he says.

"Better us than them."

Lighting strikes off my heels, picking up instant full speed, running the length of the roof then zooming off the edge into the air. Shoes melting on fire.

"Ahhhhhhhh," we shout, shooting like a bullet into the sky past the next building and the next and the next then crash landing onto a smaller building three blocks away. Going faster and farther than I expected.

We tumble, roll, and stop. It's quiet. The sky is clear.

"You *are* growing stronger," Tanz says.

I smile, lifting him and looking for a staircase.

GATHERING AT THE SAFE HOUSE

WITH EYE WATERING speed, I carry Tanz through a back alley of broken glass and garbage past a homeless family huddling together. Newspapers and plastic bags swirl in our wake. The family huddles closer, a father trying to protect them. With our passing the man's arms spread wider.

Upstairs in the rear of the safe house I place Tanz against the wall a few feet from where the roof caved in and sky is exposed. Rafters slope above wooden plank flooring.

He's groggy and weak. "I'll retrieve the bags and iron crystals. Get you strong again." I zoom out past the family. A few blocks away I skip over the ten-foot garden fence as if skipping over a stick. Apple and cherry trees sway as space and time bend.

Grabbing our bags from behind the bush I pause, inhaling deeply for a moment. It's peaceful, dark, while a few stars sparkle dimly above. The fragrance of tulip and rose fill the air. I wonder about my home out there, far away.

Back at the safe house Tanz has propped himself against a brick pile in the corner partially hidden by shadows. A yellow moon hangs low over the city. Reaching for the crystals in the bag he shakes the plastic container.

He pops two pills and hands me two. "Getting low."

Pulling out his cell phone, he presses a button. "Good evening, M. This is T. Sorry to call so late... Thank you for understanding... Dubious times indeed... I'd like to place a carry out order. Double... Yes, double... How soon? Yes, I know to order ahead of time, that it's not easy to get... It will be a few days, I understand. Thank you. Good night, M." He flips his thin phone closed and lays his head back.

"Um, who was that?" I ask, standing near him.

"A contact uptown."

I peer at him with hands out to my side.

"Oh, a provider, one who gives humans hope. An evolved human," he says, tucking the container into a pouch. Within seconds his pale eyes have grown brighter, more alert against the shadows of moonlight.

Safe, thickness now leaves my body. I relax, making sure to sit along the wall this time.

Tanz rifles through his bag again. "Here." He sticks out his hand with an individual size Tupperware and plastic spoon.

"Vegetarian chili, I warmed it up in my domicile prior to receiving a punch to my face. It is true, everyone does have a plan until they get punched in the face… Still warm," he says, smiling, crumbling up crackers.

"Thank you." He does amaze me, this man. This stranger. I eat wondering about Narican, my family, and what it means to be Sun Clan. A faint sense of Jintara hangs from a distant murky memory. A smile. A spear. Running. Laughter. Playing.

"I'm sorry I never asked, but do you have any family? You know all about me, but I don't know anything about you."

Setting down his meal, he says, "Yes, a wife. She too was an accountant."

He brightens at the idea of her. Sitting up in pain presenting images of love and joyous equations upon their ceiling while lying on the floor of their home as they figured out the universe.

"Well, is she here? Maybe the cleansing has worn off and we can find her."

"No, she is not. We had even picked out names for our child." He shows images of her pregnant and them running with him trying to save her. "Struck down by a dark blade of mist, the same as your father. She was murdered."

She disappears into the mist like ash from a fire. He continues with the imagery and different parts of the scene. He pauses, touching her face.

I look away as the image fades. My privilege saved me and got her killed. I feel alone in this cold city. Jan and Robert were also killed because of me. Sadness sweeps over me, tears fall. Tanz looks on.

"It is not your fault, Claremone. Forces exist beyond us."

I stand and pace between the shadows of moonlight. "I'm so sorry, Tanz." Anger grows at my past powerlessness, ineptitude, ignorance.

"This stops with us… no matter what. But we have nothing to go on. Nothing. I saw you couldn't get to Qualmsy. I know you tried." I kick debris in my path as if it had something to do with this.

"We failed." In the moonlight I stop pacing and clench my fist, raising it to the sky. "*Why?* What do you want of us?"

Tanz gazes upon me with the same affection he looked upon his wife. "If we'd had our child, I'd want him or her to be like you. Thank you for asking, however, I did not need to reach Qualmsy to read him."

"You didn't?"

"I touched the man you refer to as Tattoo in the same location Qualmsy had touched him when I unceremoniously entered the room. Let us look together… Come, sit…" Tanz stares at me with fatherly eyes as he pats the floor next to him.

He begins the scene when Qualmsy laughs, leaning on Tattoo. We then enter Qualmsy's DNA traces and see him leaning into the window of a black tinted limousine earlier in the day, and an exchange of cash. We cannot see a face. There are government plates on the car as it zooms away.

"83% Complete." Tanz leans back while the equation fades.

All he says is, "The chain maker…"

Silence fills the air as the decaying building settles.

"We must visit the capital," he says, rubbing his chin.

"But what about Qualmsy and his goons?"

"Once we chop off the head, the body is soon disoriented. We will return and chop it apart," he says with unflinching warrior eyes that glow, staring off into the darkness. Under his breath, I hear him say, "For you, my love."

THE DEMON TRAIN RIDE

WE HOP ON an early morning train packed with passengers out of Main Street Station to head for the capital. The conductor looks at our tickets and escorts us to seats at the front of the train. A window on the right looks upon tracks and the dark tunnel ahead while the left window shows only graffiti. The brakes release and the train heaves forward. Now rolling under Big City, the steel cars jostle, picking up speed down the tunnel.

I glance back at people reading newspapers, playing on phones, sleeping. I lean over to Tanz and say, "I'm sure Qualmsy's boss knows we escaped."

He nods, unfolding his newspaper. "We must count on that."

"Kimbel is running for Citizen Leader. How interesting," Tanz says. The paper displays color pictures of him fighting a bear, showing off his chest chopping wood.

"Whatever happened to content and good judgment? Perception is harder than thinking." He pauses. "Where are the evolved ones to lead this blind race?"

"Are there aligned ones?" I ask. "Higher humans?"

"Yes, a few."

"How do you become one?"

"I do not. But for them—" he shrugs over his shoulder to the car behind us—"it is simple, so simple really, though they find it near impossible. Flow downstream with one's consciousness and they shall arrive at an enlightened state. Be aligned with source, the soul's energy signature. One's true path. The beacon planted in them for that. If only they would listen. Not muddle through a filter of fear. Really, it is a refusal of these distractions and restrictions. Simply do not honor the fear and the reduction of one's character."

Tanz folds the paper, placing it meticulously on his lap. "Wake me when we get there," he says, closing his eyes.

I nod and stare out the window. The train bounces out of the tunnel under the river and into the next province. For several minutes we pass decaying buildings, rundown warehouses, through an area that used to bustle, now empty.

A world of wonder opens as we dive into its splendor. The landscape is a natural world of fields and forests rolling down from rugged rolling hillsides thick with thigh high country grass. An hour passes, my eyes fixed upon the exciting terrain, *there are evolved ones here.* I wonder who.

In school we learned this land was quarantined after an unknown explosion, and the Citizen Leader office deemed it uninhabitable. It's why those buildings were abandoned, water supply fouled. Strange inexplicable events happen here unsuitable for the common citizen. Or so we've been told. There are no towns between Big City and the capital.

Nature reclaimed this area decades ago with the occasional chimney still standing and red barn fallen on its side. Farmland poisoned. A no man's land of marauders, outcasts, and renegades. Rumor has it they live in these hills, in caves, and are dangerous.

The train is a nonstop between Big City and the capital. No stations wait in between.

*

We come over a pass and the view stretches for miles along a valley floor up to the next rocky hillside.

Up in the distance a dark storm hovers over the horizon, subduing the sun. Darkness spreads, feathering out. Swaths of trees sway in the distance, their wills bent by some unseen force snapping them upright as wind rolls down the hillside straight for us. The capital is in that direction.

Tanz snores and mutters recipe ingredients, "Add a tablespoon of olive oil and a pinch of salt for eureka, a delicious casserole." Expressions of interest spread across his face. I feel bad elbowing him. He startles and scowls.

Out the side window the day is still untouched by this incoming monster.

As we approach its body climbs higher, spreading further. Clouds swirl and spin.

Tanz knocks on the conductor door next to us. The bearded man with a black pony tail gives him a thumbs up then goes faster.

Darkness and wind hurl over the terrain. The train moves full speed as the storm tumbles in a fury, tearing up land. Tanz bangs on the locked door again and raises his hands, motioning for the conductor to slow down. The man points to his watch as if staying on time, offering another thumbs-up.

Wind rips up the track in front of us. Boards, one by one, right at us. Wood planks and six-inch spikes fly like daggers, cracking the window and impaling the car's steel membrane. Spears miss my face by a foot. I now see the body of this beast towering as I press my face against the window. A twister forms at the storm's front. But there's no rain. Darkness trails behind the cyclone as if pushing it, directing it.

"We're going to hit it," I say.

Tanz's eyes scan the storm like a camera lens adjusting and accounting.

"I cannot see inside this mass. Brace yourself."

I wedge my feet in front and hand against the sidewall.

The tornado pulls back then lurches forward, rushing us. Remaining tracks fly off as if we're playing chicken with the Devil.

The sound is fierce like some angry god coming down to smite us for our wicked deeds. Darkness fills every window and crevice. The angry storm smashes full force into the car like a pissed off bull. The impact lifts the rear of the car knocking people out of seats. The car smashes back to the ground wobbling. Another hit comes. Still moving forward, the train teeters another hundred yards then tips. Gravity pulling at it.

The sound is like a great ship on the sea creaking and listing after hitting an iceberg, metal peeling and bending.

"We're going over!" I say, wedging myself in.

Crashing down now skidding on our right side over jagged rocks and dirt. Luggage tumbles from racks above. Sandwiches go airborne. People fly through the air and fall into aisles. My grip slips. I smack against the now horizontal conductor door and grab the bar above, swinging from it as the train continues on. Tanz bounces off the wall landing on luggage below.

Scraping the earth, the train skids, bouncing along. In the chaos, screams fill the car. Balancing my feet, I scan the disarray. Momentum slowing, I balance my feet shifting with the heaving train.

Wind can't run into a train. Not like that. I look at the tickets and us in the front seat of the front car. Then I hear the noise as the train lurches to a stop. Metal peels and shreds as the tin can above is ripping open.

People scream, running to the rear. A few people near us are ripped out into the cyclone's body and darkness beyond as Tanz and I stumble to the rear of the car.

A black, impenetrable sky hovers. Branches and luggage swirl, potato chips float past. Man, I'm hungry. I look into the darkness and swear I can hear voices. Then we both peer at something grayish white descending from way up high. It begins taking shape. We look at each other.

Jagged canine teeth the size of a Toyota pierce the black, grinding down onto the train and chewing up the interior and metal of the car.

"That's no wind…" Tanz shouts.

"What do we do?"

"Run!"

With others we run into the back. Teeth behind us like PAC-MAN. Ripped out seats and train chunks pass into the wind chomping and sucking everything up. Still the wind spins, wrappers and papers hit me in the face. A businessman's combover blows from side to side. Luggage and people swirl above into the wind.

More people near us are swallowed by the hungry storm. The train finally lurches to a stop with one big bang. We're thrown summersaulting through the air into the darkness. The cyclone teeth dart in our direction. About fifteen of us land hard on a grass field.

The train wreckage is immense. People are down and injured and the landscape is littered with train debris. It all seems so out of place.

I look for a safe house, cave, tuft of tress, anything to hide within. The teeth at the center of the wind descend over Tanz and I. Running over I punch one tooth that breaks off and is sucked into the vortex. Another tooth pops right into place.

The mouth opens wide to bite.

"Run, Claremone."

I look up the hill in front of me and in all directions. "To where?" I shout back. The wind noise is fierce. "There's no cover. There's nowhere to go!"

Tanz shakes his head, looking up at the storm, then points. *"Ruuuunnnn!"*

It takes me a second then I nod, knowing what he means.

I scan the tornado's size. My feet start pumping, pistons firing. I lift off and run as hard as I can. First around the train then up around the wind in the opposite direction moving faster and faster as the thermals draw me along. I grind my teeth. I have to do this. I run harder and harder. I hear pain and crying from within the cyclone. Those same voices I've heard before. The storm shifts, trying to shake me off like a bucking bronco. I run faster, outpacing it. The tornado tail whips, trying to suck me in but no go. I step on it, burning up the air. The chomping six-foot teeth come at me and I knock another one into the vortex and keep running. The tail whips, knocking me about fifty feet. I shake my head from the blow, regaining composure.

I'm going to run even faster. So fast this thing will turn itself into a pretzel. I pedal, breathing deeply, gathering steam. And... now! I burst at it. Full steam like a meteor. It can't catch up as I create an updraft that diminishes the wind, shrinking it. It whips and bucks. I move faster and harder. The blackness fades and the storm shrinks. A glimmer of sunlight shines.

The horizon can be seen again. I don't stop until the wind has been reduced completely. I spin around it in faster rotations then slow into a descent.

"Great job!" Tanz shouts up as I'm slowing just above him.

My piston legs prepare for a landing with sneakers burnt and crisp. I need to get new ones.

The day clears. The deadly vortex is not entirely gone. In the palm of my hand I present the small tornado to Tanz. The baby storm bounces back and forth trying to bite my hand.

I hold the mini-tornado out for him.

"Can we keep it?" I joke.

Tanz brings his face closer, staring at it with his radiant blue eyes. The wind straightens up, standing still.

Tanz analyzes it. "This is a very sophisticated attack beyond any mortal capabilities. And whomever can control the elements. We must be wary." He places information into his equation. "87% complete." It closes and evaporates. He brings out a small box from his backpack and places the wind inside.

We check if we can help the wounded, spinning in all directions, but people are gone. No one lays in the field. Only luggage and train debris. We stare at each other and shrug.

Beginning at the rear of the train we check from seat to seat. Each person is frozen in different poses: drinking coffee, taking pictures of the landscape, reading the newspaper. We look at each other as we walk through this strange scenario. I poke a man with a newspaper. Tanz pokes a girl with a lollipop.

"They're mannequins, plastic…" Tanz says.

We stare at each other again then up and down the car. The plastic people all have looks of intrigue and enthusiasm.

One blond woman stares off with sadness in her large round eyes as a tear runs down her cheek.

"Hello, ma'am? Ma'am?" I lean in. But nothing. No blink. No breath. "All fakes? How? They were real when we left."

We get to the conductor and he too is just a beefy mannequin with beard and brown hair, plastic smile, conductor hat and thumbs up on his hand.

"Another set up. Some computer program or illusion." Tanz says confounded.

I am thoroughly confused. But I trust what I saw. "I guess that's why we were in front."

He nods.

We grab our stuff. "Might as well start walking," I say.

Back outside we see the capital off in the distance.

"Clearly someone doesn't want us to get there," Tanz says.

After some distance I look back. The train damage is severe as it lays on its side off the tracks, metal peeled away. The wreck is no illusion. Shirts and pants from open luggage rest on the ground.

*

We walk a few miles and stop with the darkness of night. It's a grassy area we tamp down into beds. Luckily, it's a warm summer's evening. We're not prepared for camping though. I find rocks to make a firepit while Tanz rummages around his bag for the little food he brought. I make the teepee for the fire out of twigs and dry grass using matches Tanz brought along.

"Is there anything you don't have in that bag?"

"No," he says, handing me a protein bar. "All natural, no preservatives…"

I nod, ravenous for anything. We rest on the grass beds trying to relax.

I start hearing those voices again, the ones I heard from within the tornado. People murmuring in pain. Different voices. A collection of them.

I listen closer and faintly hear certain words from within the myriad.

"Why did they do that to me?"

"God, I hate myself."

"You're a terrible mother. I hate you."

More grumbling and pain. Vague words about lies and killing.

"Kill you."

"Kill you."

"Kill you."

With goosebumps tickling my neck, I ask Tanz, "I'm not going crazy, right? You hear that."

He nods, scanning in all directions. "A deaf man could hear that."

"But where are they?" I ask, looking around.

"Trapped entities enslaved by the dark forces."

"Are they people?"

He purses his lips and shifts his head, pondering. "Many of them. Or their essence."

"Can they be freed? They're in pain."

"Yes, once the yoke is broken. If not, they will remain forever trapped. Forever in agony."

"How is the air filled with them? I don't understand."

He pulls up a calculation. "Their pain was somehow captured and infused within the air molecules."

The starless black sky rumbles. But no clouds rest above. Just a thick black mat.

"Is the sky also part of this?"

"Indeed, it must be. My summation is that the program controls the sky and everything beneath it."

"Controlling the elements, huh? I don't like it."

"Neither do I."

An uneasy feeling sits around us. There's no safety out here. The air is thick and heavy. Miles and miles of open terrain and clearly something is watching us, wanting something from us.

I try sleeping with one eye open but hear these rising voices murmur.

After a few minutes I push off the ground. "I can't sleep with all this racket!" I shout, tired of it. "Reveal yourself!"

Tanz rolls over pressing himself up. "Clearly they want something from us."

"Who?" I ask as he feeds the fire more grass that lights up the sky.

"Whoever is behind this. The dark forces take on many shapes. Fears you may have. Weaknesses they hope to exploit."

What he says triggers a memory of camping with my parents when I was young. After hearing noises in the woods, I got so scared I thought a bear was outside our tent cracking twigs and rustling leaves. I thought he was going to eat us and only our bones would be left. I laid in the tent paralyzed by fear. It turned out to be a raccoon rustling through smores trash.

Tanz hands me a few iron core crystals.

"That's the last of it. We will acquire more from my contact when we return and continue reconnecting strands."

"And if we ever want to get home, right?"

"Yes, that as well."

Feeling stronger, I stand. The moaning voices continue as my anger grows.

"Come on! We're right here!" I shout at them.

Their volume and anger grows, matching mine.

"Do not encourage them. Anger begets anger. We are somehow on their land. In their lair if you will."

I think about this land that had been closed to the public. For testing perhaps. I wonder if this is a trap and if Tanz knows that too.

"We're in trouble out here, aren't we? I mean, there's no safe space for miles. Kind of at their mercy."

"As always we are safe in the moment remaining one with our highest selves aligned with universal intelligence. And yet of course I see your point."

"We're not sleeping anyway. Let's go check it out. See what they want. I'd be having nightmares anyway if I was."

We stomp out the small fire then cover it with rocks.

We walk a few feet in each direction, seeing nothing.

"Well, which way?" I ask, then a horrible voice shrieks behind me. *"Boo."* I jump.

"They're just trying to scare us…" Tanz says.

"Well, it's working."

The voice shrieks again like bones had broken and a scream follows. Scratchy voices flood the empty landscape like bodiless ghosts.

"They want us to move westward," Tanz says.

I nod, stumbling over a rock and landing on the hard-packed soil. "I'm getting sick of this! What do you want?" I shout again, propped up on the ground.

"Yyyyoouuuuu," I hear. Chills run through me.

"Did you hear that, Tanz?"

"How could I not?" he says as we continue walking.

A glow appears in the distance under the matte black sky. A bright red glow that radiates heat. I get warmer, the heat intensifies. As we approach, I see Tanz clearly, as bright as daylight, with the dark sky and rugged landscape around us.

"This appears as if a mirage," he says.

"Mirages aren't hot," I say as we slow our pace.

The heat source comes into sight. We stop atop a small bowl maybe fifty yards in length. Gnarled oddly shaped leafless trees stand petrified around the perimeter.

"Is that… lava?" I ask, peering down in confusion.

Tanz calculates. "It cannot be, though appears so. However, no active lava beds exist in the east let alone within miles of the capital. These are all programs. False realities."

"You can't feel programs, Tanz. So, what do we do? I mean, we've come this far."

"Enter, I suppose. It is the only way to learn."

With better judgment, I plead, "But I don't really want to enter and learn. I have a bad feeling about this."

"As we are meant to."

"That's really great, Tanz. Comforting. I'm feeling so much *worse* now. Thank you."

"Any time."

We walk down the slope of the bowl into the small valley. The lava lake sits about thirty feet into the center where the land is flat. The lava appeared calm when we stood at the top but now bubbles and spits flames as we descend. The voices and cries of pain vanish from the air.

Across on the far hillside a crow lands on a tree branch and is instantly fried, ashing over, dusting to the ground. Another one lands, the branch moves like an arm and the bird is eaten at the tip, sucked right in.

"Did you see that? That branch just ate that bird."

But Tanz didn't see. He's looking at the glowing red pool in front of us, calculating with a fading blue equation.

"My sight is distorted here," he says, when a shrill cry calls out from within the bowl, echoing.

"This was definitely a bad idea."

"Yes, by my calculations I would have to agree with you."

"What did it say?"

"You don't want to know. Low possible outcome."

I nod, growing more uncertain with each step.

Once we reach the base of the hill the top tree branches begin extending out from all sides toward the center of the bowl. Roots shoot down the hill from the lowest part of the trees. These roots have come alive, slithering down the hillside toward us.

"Look, they're snakes." I point. A high pitch shriek permeates the bowl.

"Ah, they're playing," Tanz says as the slithering roots snap at each other.

"And the branches are closing off the top. Snakes and branches, your little equation couldn't see that?"

"No, it could not. Clearly they anticipate us to dust and disappear. That bird was an example," Tanz observes. "That is why they lured us down here. To disappear."

The branches at the top closest together begin connecting as the middle ones extend toward the center.

The snake roots get closer, shriek louder, and the lava lake rumbles.

I cover my ears as the roof is closing and sky shrinking. "Why has it gotten so loud?"

"This is a game to them." He draws up another calculation that quickly fades. "I cannot hold them. My ability, this extra sense. My DNA is unraveling within my cells," he says, losing the waving blue images.

"It's time we get out of here anyway. Watch this." I grab Tanz.

The branches almost complete their connection across the center, blocking out the sky as if forming a newly thatched hut. My feet begin pulsating and pumping. My legs thicken and I grow strong, but with a slight cramp, tightness in my right leg. As we lift off, I pump harder and the pistons sound and jet engine blares. We rise above the snapping snakes and move for the hilltop and trees.

My legs sputter as the cramp grows, tightening like a Charlie Horse. The pistons stutter and jet engine coughs like a struggling motor. I try willing them. We move upward but not fast enough. My legs spin but I feel them slowing, losing thickness. My grip on Tanz weakens. I cannot hold it.

Tanz shouts into my ear, "You can't make it! The iron and nickel in the lava are zeroing out the iron crystals in our blood."

Losing to gravity, dropping several feet out of control.

"It's our only chance." I pump harder, calming my mind. *Align with my higher self, align with my higher self.*

The jet engine roar returns as we shoot up, slamming into the roof branches—bending but not breaking them. Our momentum stops, my body slackens, and I drop Tanz. We tumble through the air approaching the ground fast. Snake roots await, ready to strike, snapping up at us. We hit the ground with a hard thud.

We slap several roots away with our hands. He shoots laser eyes. A few recoil but the laser shorts out.

"Tanz, Tanz, are you okay?" I ask, rushing over to him. Several fangs jut out around him.

"Fine. I'm fine." They surround us, hissing and snapping.

I look up. "Look, the roof is closed. I can't see the sky."

A clicking sound echoes as if the wood is interlocking in place one by one, sealing up the bowl and hillside. The trees now come alive beneath the roofline. Multiple eyeballs pop out of openings where birds and other creatures must have poked holes. Some trees have only one or two. Larger ones have a dozen or more eyes darting about, staring at us from the bowl perimeter like watchmen.

"We have to get out of here, Tanz. But how? You're the brains of this operation."

"Can you run?"

"You mean, like, jog? I can try but don't see how that's going to work," I say, looking up at the defenses waiting for us.

"Focus on the young ones. They can't see as well. You take the lead. I'll run behind you. There." He points to two thin, short trees with one eye each. I look at him like he's crazy.

"The only way out of here is up." He looks back at the lava while batting away another root. "Unless you want to go in there," he says.

"What about you?"

"I can run. I'm not that old. On the count of three."

"Okay. Okay," I say, as there appears no other options.

"One, two, three!" I take off at a sprint.

Tanz on my rear is keeping up.

"Not bad, old man."

"Not bad yourself," he says huffing as we dig into the hillside.

As a human I dig hard. Legs not thickening. The top of the hill is not far but steep. I begin huffing and puffing, zigzagging between snakes halfway up. Another few feet and we almost make it to the lip and base of the trees.

"Come on." I grab his hand, pulling him.

I pump hard trying to build momentum when snake roots strike us. One nips me on the arm and my skin sizzles. Another hits Tanz from the side. He lets out a sigh of pain and we both tumble down the hill. Now laying on top of hardened roots that are still moving toward the center. The only open space left will be the lava pool.

"They seem less interested in us now than in connecting." I say.

They pass along the ground under us. The shrieks have paused. We stand brushing ourselves off.

"If they connect, we're dead…"

"This is a mouth," Tanz says.

"What are we supposed to do?"

Tanz pauses. "Past the trees is our only escape. Or is that what we are to believe? Give me a moment."

"We don't have a moment!" A root grabs my left hand then another grabs my right. They wrap tightly around, pulling me toward the lava.

"I can't fight it. Too strong. *Grrr.*" I try pulling loose but can't.

A root slides between my legs attempting to connect with incoming roots. I step down hard on it. It stops slithering, snaps, and bites me on the thigh. My skin sizzles and smokes. It burns like acid.

"Don't do that!" Tanz implores.

I nod, having already figured that out. One grabs Tanz and drags him toward the lava pool. "I. Can't. Stop. It."

"The lava's bubbling higher!" I shout above the noise.

He responds, "Whomever is killing us intends to leave no trace of us. We will burn up and ash away with history." Tanz stares at me as the root pulls him closer. "It is feeding time," he says with his low measured voice.

We're trapped. The root snakes have slithered around, encasing us like a wooden jail. I see how far we are to the lava through a sliver between the snake cage bars. The shrill cries pierce the air as they draw us near.

Tanz shouts above the snake frenzy. "…If the nickel and iron of the lava can zero out and neutralize the iron core crystals, well then, the same must be true in the opposite direction. And lastly, I never told you, but I hate snakes. They do not exist on Narican."

"Great to know. Well, how do you propose we do that?" I'm sweating from the heat of the lava. Too hot. "Tanz, hurry up. I'm starting to cook."

"I have no calculations. Just a theory. Blood. Find a sharp root or snake tooth and cut yourself. Aim or rub it on the root. The immune system built into our blood will attack anything impure." He lets out a scream as the root squeezes tighter. Bones may break.

"I hope this works," I say.

"If not, we have failed."

"And are gonna die."

"Yes, we will die. As will Narican."

I find a sharp root and cut my hand and forehead on a snake tooth. The blood drips and the parts of the root disintegrate and loosen. More blood drips and the roots smoke.

"It's working," I say as the snake root cries out in pain, retreating. My ears are hurting. "Worst... Sound... Ever...!"

We can't get close enough to the lava, but a hole is created in the roots. We fall out as they retreat.

A few feet away we stand and stare at each other then start spitting at the lava. Roots begin coming at us again, striking. We slap them away. Steam rises where the spit hits. Small stones now float. I spit some more.

Standing so close we perspire heavily, wiping our brows and shaking our hands, throwing whatever sweat and spit we have left. More chunks of stone form on the surface.

"It's not enough..." I say. My mouth growing dry. Snakes slither faster down the hillside.

"What else can we do? They're coming," I say, staring at them then Tanz.

He ponders for a moment. "We must pee into it."

"What?"

"It is the only fluid left we can spare. Now pee into it!" he commands.

Now that he mentions it, I have been holding it a while.

"Fine, but don't look, okay?" I turn away, unzipping.

"I won't, but shake it around." We stream pee in all directions.

"Don't waste any. Get as close as you can."

I step closer to the lava edge trying not to fall in. Feeling like a firefighter: Code 12. Code 12 Lava Lake with snake roots: hose running at full strength.

On a side note, I've always been known to have a large bladder yet never thought it could save my life.

More stones pop up. The lake rumbles, turning gray. The lava bed steams and settles. I shake what's left. "Now that felt good," I say, zipping my pants.

The last rock spits up and rolls within a few feet of us. The heat diminishes. The snake roots retreat up the hillside, snapping at each other. The roof retracts and opens.

Breathing heavily, we look at each other, catching our breaths, sweating.

"Might as well bed down for the night here," he says. Exhausted from the battle and hunger, we fall asleep next to the lava bed seeing the night sky again. Stars are plentiful.

*

The next morning is sunny. We walk up and out of the bowl. I stop at a petrified tree and think I hear it hiss. Snapping off a branch I throw it as far as I can. The branch smashes into pieces on the jagged stone lava below.

We find our way back to the government road and continue toward the capital. The strange voices are gone. A few miles pass and we see the tips of the capital's tallest buildings off on the horizon. We're getting closer. My stomach grumbles.

"I am so hungry."

"We'll find something in the capital."

That idea settles me for the moment.

In the barrenness of our surroundings, something is out of place. A bicyclist rides from the direction of the capital, fast, as if propelled at us by a motor.

"Keep an eye out." Tanz says.

The man slows then stops on the other side of the road clearly keeping his distance. His right hand remains on a small lever.

"Nice day for a walk," he says, looking around then up at the sky and back down at us. "Where are you guys going?" He's fit with wavy blond hair and blue eyes, early thirties.

"To the capital…" Tanz answers.

"Let me guess, a couple of darkness salesmen: guns, mind manipulation, murder. Not enough pain in the world for you?"

"No, sir. We're just tourists. And you are?" Tanz responds.

He points and says, "Just a bicyclist enjoying a sunny day and fresh air. You see that dark cloud hanging over the capital? It's been growing in recent months, yet the capital is always sunny."

"How can that be?" I ask.

"You tell me." He looks us over. "You two may not be darkness pushers, but you sure aren't tourists either. It's a strange town. You've been warned."

"We're getting used to strange."

"Whatevs. Enjoy the walk. They do have faster ways of *geeetttt-ttting thee-eeerrrre…*" He presses the lever and the bike shoots away at breakneck speed as if his ten-speed had a jetpack. A second later he cruises over a hill we passed half a mile back.

We stand alone on the road that carves out this strange rugged wilderness leading us to answers, and no doubt, trouble. Hopefully some food first.

"Weird stuff out here, Tanz..."

"And the weirdness will most likely increase."

Another hour of walking with tired feet and we make it to the capital gates and city limits. A black cloudless sky sits overhead.

THE WEIRD CAPITAL, FOOD,
AND A POLITICIAN

INSIDE THE GATES, row houses run up to the edge but not beyond, not into no man's land.

"Wait a sec." I walk back outside the gates.

"There's a black sky above but it's sunny inside," I say, walking back in.

"As the man said," Tanz runs a quick equation. "It is the same black sky that yesterday sat over the lava lake and the day before dictated the storm and tornado." He wipes it aside.

"So, what do we do about it?"

"Nothing at the moment. The universe has a way of revealing information when needed."

"Great. Can it reveal some food?"

"Let us walk."

A few blocks in we act like tourists, pointing out famous buildings, taking goofy pictures. In front of the Grand Almeida building there is a brick square with several food trucks. I walk over to the hot dog stand and overhear Tanz say behind me, "Selfie." He snaps a picture of himself then types into his phone.

"What are you doing?" I shout over.

"Posting to InstaFace."

I cram my mouth with ketchup laced hot dogs.

Tanz takes a more tactful approach to eating and chewing, with measured bites. "Good for the digestive tract."

Everyone in the square is happy and smiling. There are jugglers, balloon guys, children chasing bubbles, people sitting on walls reading. I start feeling lightheaded myself. I'd like to juggle for a while or lay down, nap on the grass as several others are doing.

Tanz looks at me with scowling, intense eyes.

"Why are you so unhappy?" I ask him.

We look at each other strangely. My head doesn't feel right. We look back to where we'd been. The hillsides surrounding the city are sunny.

"Come." Tanz pulls me by the hand.

"Why, this is so great."

We walk back outside past the gates; the dark cloud looms overhead.

"Breathe… get your senses about you. I cannot continue with you acting like a buffoon."

My happiness fades outside the city gates, back to my old self. I shake my head. Tanz slaps me on the shoulders.

"Okay, okay, what was that?"

"Stay here." He steps onto the other side of the gate and tests the air with a small equation in his hands, so no one sees him. It concludes, folds, and flies off.

"There's a slight drug in the air putting everyone in this euphoric state. A compression chamber envelopes the city."

"You mean a bubble?"

"Precisely, a bubble."

"The black sky is creating that?"

"It is more like something is creating the black sky."

"Why?"

"The illusion of joy is too overwhelming to ignore. People often seek to escape their struggles with a misperception of happiness. Do not get lost in it again. Stay focused on your heart and spirit when we re-enter; this will keep your head from floating off."

I store the information away as we step back in.

"Okay, so how are we going to find this politician?"

"Like anyone else, call him." He brings up an image that shimmers radiant blue.

"I see you've gotten your DNA back."

"One must align one's cells with source. Thus, allowing one's higher self."

"I'm starting to get it."

He scans an image of Qualmsy then scrolls back to earlier, in the limousine. Qualmsy seems uptight, straightening his back in his red velvet room with the floating haze balls above him. He stares at the phone as if someone is yelling at him. Tanz zooms in on the number across the phone screen and reads his moving lips. "Se-na-tor Kim-bel." Tanz mouths along with Qualmsy.

"The guy from the newspaper?"

"Ah, the ego. Apparently fighting bears is not enough."

Tanz grabs the phone out of his pocket and dials. It rings several times and it doesn't seem like he's going to pick up. About to click off, we finally hear, "Hello."

Tanz doesn't respond yet closely listens. I lean in.

"Hello, who is this?"

"Ah, Senator Kimbel, we are looking for you. Are you, sir, scared of the boogey man? Well the boogey *men* have arrived." He takes the phone away from his ear and snickers. I roll my eyes.

"How did you get this number? Is *this* the old man? I heard you had escaped my associate." Tanz places it on speakerphone and we listen. There's typing in the background. "I hope you brought the boy..."

"Oh, he would not miss a chance to visit the capital and our favorite senator."

"Soon to be Citizen Leader. Good. We've been waiting for you."

"Oh, and thank you for sending your welcoming committee outside the city. Very impressive. Lava. We'll be visiting with *you* real soon." Tanz clicks off, not picking up anything certain, and shakes his head.

We keep walking into the capital toward the city center.

"Wow, you talk a good game, man."

"I do understand the finer details of smack talking and its effectiveness."

*

On the main road there are many people and television monitors everywhere on lampposts, shop windows, street corners floating for people to view while walking, at bus stops and in some places embedded in the concrete of the sidewalk.

At a storefront we stop to watch. Though summertime, two women walk in fur coats and also stop to watch. There is a montage of Senator Kimbel running for Citizen Leader.

The beautiful blonde newscaster exclaims what a great citizen he's been.

"What a lucky nation we are. And this newscaster hopes upon hopes that he becomes our next Citizen Leader. We now take you to this exalted candidate's press conference."

His press secretary stands at the podium. "Ladies and gentlemen, without further ado, your candidate and soon to be Citizen Leader, Senator Kimbel!"

The crowd goes wild and gives a standing ovation as he walks onto the stage.

One of the women in a fur coat says, "He's so manly, like a handsome knight."

"So strong and smart. I wish my husband were more like him," the other one agrees.

The clip shifts to Kimbel chopping wood, bench pressing without a shirt on, signing bills into law, helping old ladies across the street, and saving cats from trees. After the vain montage, back on the stage he stands as the ovation fills the auditorium with reverie as if a savior has come to deliver them. His stunning blonde wife stands next to him as he waves. Banner slogans roll across the monitor bottom. *"Our Country is Boldest with Kimbel."*

"Impressive," Tanz says.

Across the street a haze ball enters a sewer grate. "They're watching us," I say, elbowing him.

Scoping each direction of the city, he creates a small equation. "By the size of the place, Kimbel must have trackers around the perimeter and more heavily concentrated in the center. I calculate a thousand trackers, haze, and dark forces to watch his enemies."

"That would be us, right?"

"Yes. And as they say in politics: keep your friends close, and enemies closer."

"I'm glad I'm not in politics."

"We are all in politics, like it or not."

We walk farther toward the city center and state house. People watch us on street corners then evaporate and float off.

"How can they do that?" I ask. "How are we supposed to know if someone is real or not? Same as the people on the train."

"We won't. If we smell sulfur, trust it's them. If so, run. Don't stare. They will attack. There are too many of them."

We walk and more images flash of reverent staged pictures doing more manly things: fishing, catching a burglar.

The newscaster fawns over him, "What an amazing man!"

Tanz observes, "It is a package they're selling like blue jeans or a bag of potato chips that will change your life, but not make you fat…"

As we walk on, I look down at my waist wondering how blue jeans would make me fat.

Tanz stops, putting up his hand in front of me the way my mother and father used to when hitting the car brakes. Haze clusters gather at the next intersection.

"We must be getting close," I say.

The ticker across the monitors read CITIZEN LEADER CANDIDATE KIMBEL LEAVES PRESS CONFERENCE. He gets into a limousine, the same one from Qualmsy's.

People smile on the street, looking at storefront monitors and windows waiting for busses or just staring at the brave and powerful images, probably feeling so safe and secure, happy. A reflection of colors flash in one man's captivated face. Images project from the lamppost he's entranced with.

His dilated eyes and joyous facial expression bounce along with every flashing image then with a sudden burst the colors reflected in his face are flat, solid, dark. He double takes, looking at us with anger.

The newscaster reports, "Just a moment ago—" she holds her earpiece—"this ungodly event happened."

All monitors switch. All images on the sets are now of Tanz and I murdering Senator Kimbel in his limousine as if it already happened. People on the street see us strangling, striking him.

"But, Tanz, that didn't happen. We wouldn't…" I stop speaking as people turn at us in anger, closing in. We walk faster.

As the newscaster speaks the volume on all sets increase. "If you see this old man and boy they are wanted for the murder of our most beloved and soon to be Citizen Leader." Visibly shaken, the newscaster dabs her eyes with a tissue.

"Just a few months ago we lost Senator Milleron under similar pretenses. Now our most beloved Senator Kimbel is dead. These senseless murders must stop."

Streaming headlines of "MURDERERS!" are on every television, seen by every face. Quickly we move down the block, but the mob closes in. The man whose face went from joy to hatred grabs me as others grab Tanz.

"They killed our leader!"

"Rip them to shreds!"

They're pulling and yanking my arms as the police arrive. Placed in a squad car, we're hauled away. Their faces all filled with rage and hatred as we drive off.

I lean in and ask, "But what about all the joy?"

Tanz's only response, "Base emotions."

AFTER BEING CAUGHT BY THE MOB

I WAKE IN a cement room with mist spraying out of two encased sprinklers on the ceiling. Tanz is awake, studying them. "It's the toxin. Breathe through your shirt."

"The cleansing toxin?"

Tanz nods.

"But how?"

He shakes his head. "We will weaken then our DNA will break down. Must esca…" he says, passing out.

My eyes then close.

When I wake two very large men stand in the room with rippling muscles and empty, soulless black eyes like the men at Qualmsy's. The spray has stopped. Without a word they lift and throw us over their shoulders like bags of flour. I'm so weak I cannot move or tell if I am. Groggy, I'm having trouble connecting thoughts.

We're brought into a main room where Senator Kimbel waits. Busts of dead Citizen Leaders stand in a row on the side beneath portraits of war scenes and valiant generals striding atop mountainsides. He speaks, pressing his face against a strange looking device with a contoured monitor.

"You must trust me. I've dealt with far more dangerous opponents than a boy and an old man. I've bombed entire countries: wiped them off the face of the earth. A bullet works the same for them all. Excuse me, my guests have arrived." As we enter, he pushes away from the device, pulling a sheet over it.

"Welcome… Welcome…" He stands, clapping his hands together. "My mighty adversaries…" His sandy hair is perfectly parted. He wears a crisp blue collared shirt.

The big guys set us in chairs and tie us up then stand at our flanks. "Just for precautions. But by the looks of you, there is little need… However, you did elude Mr. Qualmsy. Yet the toxins are powerful and you will soon be dead."

"How long were we unconscious?" Tanz asks, rubbing his face and stubble.

"A mere three days."

Tanz's dim eyes grow wide. "Who were you speaking with?" he asks with shoulders slumped forward.

"That is no matter to you. Thank you, gentlemen," he says to the guards. "They don't speak but nod and grunt a bit. More than enough, I think. We've made them very strong empty vessels, beings incapable of guilt or remorse, so save yourself the trouble. Don't ask or think you can persuade them to help you. They cannot. With a little help we've made them physical only by withdrawing certain DNA strands: a simple process really. Their minds are capable of basic survival: food, hunger, aggression, sex."

Tanz looks over at me.

"How do you know of the toxins?" I ask, trying to right my brain.

"I know many things. One thing for certain is you will remain clouded then you will know nothing as darkness consumes your minds. I may even have you work for me. My little puppets. I have so wanted to meet you, but as you can understand it would not have been possible until now, as you are beneath my station and there had been no need. Can you imagine me spending time with a low-level accountant and a supermarket clerk?" He laughs to himself. "Absurd. I have wondered what the fuss is all about. Opponents of such high esteem, a boy and an old man." He stresses with a mocking tone, shaking his head, bursting out laughing, slapping his knees.

"So menacing. Scary indeed."

"We have names you know…" I say, trying to shake my head clear.

"Not for much longer you don't."

"But why fake your own murder?" Tanz inquires, holding up his head.

He smiles proudly. "I've never met anyone a little bad publicity couldn't kill faster than a bullet."

"But how will you run for Citizen Leader if people think you're dead?" I ask.

"The news reports will have it wrong. I was only captured but escaped. If people believe their beloved leader is dead, they will be even more impressed that I can beat death. In fact, to them I would seem godlike. Perception is reality in this city of lies."

He flips a switch and speaks into a mic on the wall intercom. "Play the video."

A large monitor on the far wall shows him breaking free. The same newscaster from earlier reports, "It's a miracle! Early accounts were wrong. Citizen Leader candidate Kimbel lives! He fought off and subdued his captives. Oh, praise the lord. Our nation is not lost." The video shows him freeing himself then beating us up and kicking out the window of the limousine.

"You can do quite a bit with video software these days. We've shot a few of them. I'm not sure which one we'll release. As you know, humans are easily led and not so evolved. Wouldn't you agree, Mr. Tanz?"

"Why, yes, in fact, I would. You are a master manipulator indeed. Impressive calculations."

I stare at Tanz and shake my head.

He stares back at me. "It is an impressive plan."

"Oh, that is the greatest compliment a foe can receive: the sign of true respect when your opponent acknowledges he is defeated."

Tanz shrugs at me.

"Oh yeah," I say, trying to sound tough, "well, we're still taking you down."

"I respect your zeal, young man, yet that will prove an impossible task. All doors are sealed for you, quite literally and figuratively. For instance, my presidential opponent is only a puppet set up by my allies to assure people that the election is fair. And we have war on monitors from trusted 'news sources.' Base fear is the root of people's decisions. If they trust that I am their protector and provider they will follow me down every dark path and whim, even if it is to kill their own mother because I showed them she was a traitor. Pitting people against each other is child's play. Pitting people against their own interests also takes little effort. Yet being a politician does have its challenges."

He pauses and sighs. "Divisiveness pays."

Kimbel smiles. "After I'm Citizen Leader the people will eat out of the palm of my hand. No, in fact I'll make them eat scraps from the floor!" He laughs. "And I will blame my enemies, saying there is no longer enough to go around."

I shout, "But that's not true!"

"They only know what I tell them, boy!" He stands, pointing at me, his tone harsh. "People succumb to fear. It rules them. It's one of the strongest human emotions. They don't want freedom. They want to be led!"

He calls someone on the phone. "Add another ten percent of the toxins to the dark forces. Get them riled up."

Tanz rights himself. "How do you know about the dark forces, sir?"

Kimbel smiles. "I told you. I know many things."

There are about a dozen monitors with faces mostly of men behind him, the heads of countries and corporations. A plaque beneath each state says who it is. All are watching this unfold.

He presses the intercom again. "Tell them to run more violence and war. Black, white, race, you know the drill."

The screens on the side walls flash more blood, buildings exploding, bloodied children and mothers in the street of some war-torn nation.

"This taps into the basest impulse of the limbic system. We create war and more policing then create more laws to ensure safety in order for people to give up their rights. As if there are constant imminent threats that would erode laws and policy to protect them. They don't understand that *we* are the ones they must fear and that *we* are the ones creating war!"

He looks at his nails and bites them. Then absently says, "I am to be king…"

"But this is a democracy!" I shout at him.

"Not of this silly country, boy, but of Earth! Don't you feel it? I can feel it. King of Earth has a nice ring to it, yes? While the only thing you two will feel is life passing before your eyes. A pleasure it has been. Now take them away!"

The beefy guys with absent eyes untie us. Kimbel puts up his hand. We stop at the door. "Once the toxins have completed breaking down your DNA we will have you on a quick trial on the news then you will be sent to prison, but really we will have you killed. An accident or something will befall you. Perhaps suicide. I've not yet decided that part of your fate."

He waves his hand. As the door closes we see him lift the sheet to that strange device.

TO THE TOXIC ROOM

STRUGGLING TO ESCAPE, but the hands of the big men are like steel vices we can't budge. They don't even shift their eyes when they throw us into a room to die. With the deadbolt locking, sprayers come on. I bang on the door but can't hear them or tell if they've walked away. I guess that also means they can't hear us scream.

I drop against the wall where Tanz is propped up.

"Take small breaths," he says.

"I'm trying to…"

We both breathe through our shirts.

He attempts an equation but it collapses like sandcastles at the beach.

"I can't hold them. I… I can't equate. We're losing strands." Popping sounds come from within us like cracking fingers. He closes his eyes and passes out, his head droops to the side.

I am getting weaker too. My eyes blurring, burning, room spinning. I feel a snapping, like rubber bands drying and breaking within me.

That woman's voice in my head speaks. *"You must save him. He is dying."*

I fight to keep my eyes open but, heavy, they shut. I ram them open again, but they close, muscles too weak. I can't raise my hands or open my eyes.

Memories of my Earth parents float in front of me, their images turning to dust. A popping in my neck causes my head to snap forward. We are going to die here.

"He does not have the warrior cells you do. Save him, Claremone. He stores and interprets our history."

The toxins gnaw on my consciousness. I keep fighting but it's winning, disorienting me. Confusion and doubts, despair and loneliness. I'm cold. So cold.

My head falls forward. I cannot lift it, but think the words, "Sun Clan, gods of light, he has saved me. I must save him. Please hear my words. I ask for your help and guidance." I slump against Tanz and pass into a dreamworld.

Floating off to the accident, I stand along the park road. The car with my parents approaches. We'd had a good day hiking. Most teens don't like spending time with their parents but I did.

I peer in and see a smile on our three faces. Then the steering wheel locks. My father fights it. The car skids. Shadows pass over me, closing in. The day turns to darkness enveloping the car. I yell but they can't hear me. I wave my arms, jump up and down, but they don't see me. Fear fills their faces. I can't help. They're losing control. I'm stupid, ignorant, doing nothing in the backseat. Nothing to save them. I jump in front of the car, but it passes right through me.

Tires squeal. Darkness spreads, I smell sulfur and know it's the evil dark forces laughing at me. The car slams into the evergreens on that empty park road. The shadows lift and sun returns. Banging on their windows. They're dead. I'm not knocked out in the backseat.

Coffins in drawers pulled from the mortuary wall. Rigor mortis that were once my parents. Painful memories buried in cells swirl around. The mortuary is filled with haze balls as doctors wearing lab coats.

Loneliness and isolation, loss and defeat. Running now with my family in the onyx palace of Narican. Fear and terror, dark forces, too many of them. My father and mother, all of them disintegrated by dark blades of mist. I lived. They died. I'm sorry. I'm so sorry I lived. I see the dark haze taking over, spreading. Narican and its people enslaved. I feel so cold. Death pulls me to join them.

"All is lost, boy. All is lost. As your life will soon be." Kimbel's voice speaks, but someone else is there, as if the palace itself has turned evil.

As the dream fades, a dark star pulsates hiding something buried deep in space.

I travel to my blood cells deep within and ride a cell inside my veins. The dream has switched again. I ride upon a red blood cell inside a running vein like a river. The river walls are turning gray. It's the toxins I realize and try paddling away from the encroaching gray. The blood behind me is hardening turning gray like the lava pool. I feel sick, achy like a fever coming on. I will myself to paddle faster pulled toward the center of my body where my soul is stored. Gray matter fills the space, organs slowing, my lungs heavy, aching, heartbeat weakening. The blood behind me is gray and hardening.

Fanged monsters pop up from hardened cells as if demons from within me, within memories. The monsters rip up chunks of gray stone that feed them as they grow larger in size with each bite. They are multiplying. The monsters rise above as I shrink in weakness.

A pool of red like an oasis with hints of star dust, my soul sparkles awaiting in front. All veins and arteries, capillaries flow in and out with enriched blood are also graying at the edges of my soul. Colors of my soul, red, green, blues flash out, pulsating. These fanged beasts grow in numbers trying to get past me.

Confusion grows as one fanged beast gets into the soul area and begins gnawing. I quickly grow confused, disoriented as to who I am. I push the beast out and regain clarity.

Cell membranes gray in all directions. The glistening pool and red cell I'm balancing on are the only red left I can see. Each bite of hardened stone pains me. The beasts gnaw on my turned blood. I try fighting them off but more appear. I kick and use my feet but am weak, tired, sleepy. I can hardly lift them.

"Save Tanz. Save yourself. It rests on you Claremone."

Tanz, oh shoot, right. I think, looking around at the situation. I forgot about Tanz and the room of toxin. His eyes closed next to me. I realize they want my soul to control me. Darken it. He saved me. I must save him. The blood cell I'm on grays and stops moving.

Snapping sounds are heard above as DNA links snap like bridges in a storm. Pieces fall of grayed stone. I clench my fist and feet, closing my eyes, focusing my mind, inhaling and blowing out one last powerful breath.

"I am Light Being... Narican Blood... Claremone of the Sun Clan," I say, emptying my lungs... *"I refuse the darkness. I say nooooooooooooooooooooo to the dark forces. I am light!"*

The ground begins rumbling. The top layers of gray stone crack and shoot up. Deep red blood fissures fire out of my soul center flooding every artery and vein. My blood begins to boil. Heat rising. Fanged beasts boil with the shooting gray stone plopping down into pure red blood. The graying walls crumble like rock faces shearing off splashing into the blood river. Red membrane walls pulsate with each new heartbeat. *Boom-boom. Boom-boom.* Splashing gray stones dissolve.

The cell that I stand upon boils. My muscles flex. Legs thicken. Focus sharpens.

My Narican cells boil the impure toxins. The soul pool overflows the banks with growing waves. A shaking and rumbling jostle me as if an earthquake.

A tidal wave rises above me. The pool of my soul grumbles angrily. My heart pounds. My skin walls shake furiously as if an eruption is taking place.

There's pain and pressure as if wood and concrete are smashing my body. The tidal wave crashes and I ride the wave's peak. I breathe choking, cold, feeling air on my skin, as if I'm in my body again.

My eyes open as I shoot thousands of feet into the sky through clouds past geese, seeing stars. I get my bearings looking down at the gaping hole in the state building roof, which gets smaller and smaller.

I shake my thoughts while shooting through the sky like a rocket. Holding Tanz, flying directionless, without guidance. We reach an apex above the cloud cover when gravity pulls us back, winning the battle. Trying to move my legs but can't. Stiff and in pain like after a bad stomach flu. We come down fast, tumbling through the air. Tanz is unconscious in my arms. We fall fast approaching the ground. I can do nothing but aim my body, straighten myself out, sticking my head forward like a skydiver without a parachute.

We come down on an angle with my toes guiding us, missing buildings, twisting my body. We crash land on a pile of cut grass inside the gates of a cemetery. We tumble and bounce. I squeeze him tight, smacking into the cement base of a mausoleum.

The wind knocks out of me. *"Ooph."* My pants are shredded, and shoes are burnt again. But we're here. On the ground. With fresh air. I make sure Tanz is breathing by listening over his mouth. It's faint. His chest is moving. He needs medical attention. I try to get up but fall down. It's night. I grow dizzy and pass out.

MUST SAVE HIM

IT'S STILL NIGHT when I wake. Tanz is next to me muttering angrily, sweating, bleeding from his forehead and hands. We need iron core crystals fast. I check the pockets of his khakis. Nothing. He'd said that was the last of it. But who did he call for more? I don't know and can't ask him. I'm weak and dizzy, propping myself up against the mausoleum base. The stars spin above. We seem to be in a more residential area. I notice high-end homes to the right, apartment buildings and storefronts in front and to the left.

I stare again at Tanz. What would he do? A splitting headache twists my eyesight. I notice again that my shoes and pants are burnt. Can't go out in public like this.

I look again at Tanz. *Necessary means,* I think. *Necessary means.* Have no choice.

"Can you stay here?"

He doesn't respond.

"Good, I'll be right back."

Hunched over, my stomach retches. I dry heave for a moment then walk onto a side road under a streetlamp past apartment buildings to find a phone booth directory. Scanning the P section, there's a pharmacy nearby. I look at the street map in front of the book and rip out the page. Pull my shirt collar up, though it's late—there shouldn't be many passersby. And if there are, hopefully they won't notice my pants hanging like window drapes and become alarmed.

I find the place and notice cars on the other side of the road with a few guys standing there watching me. It must be two in the morning. Possible dark forces.

I stare back at the four of them, not haze, but humans who look like trouble. Blue jeans, leather vest, one guy has a mohawk. I'm alone but can't worry about them right now. Tanz is dying and I may be too. There will be nothing left of Narican if we both die here.

I drag my burned feet and aching body to the store window. Red bricks surround a sapling out front. I glance at the guys but have no choice. Grabbing the brick, I smash the glass and toss it aside, quickly stepping inside to get my bearings. A few perimeter lights glow. Seeing "Pharmacy" in the rear I head back to where they store the pills. In front of large drawers, I scan the letters of the alphabet: iron, iron-multi, iron-nickel. I grab anything with iron in it snagging a reusable tote bag hanging from the closest aisle. On my way out, several waters are grabbed off shelves.

Into the main aisle sits a bin of work boots. Looking at my burnt shoes peeling off, I grab a pair and socks hanging next to them. I leave my burnt ones in exchange, walking out the way I came in.

No police come or alarm has gone off. I wonder if this is a trap. If the scouts already know we're here.

Outside on the sidewalk I peer across the street then up and down the block—the group of guys are gone. My heart beats harder thinking they may have found Tanz. Knowing he was alone. I scuffle back to the cemetery half running half limping. It's dark and Tanz is pale, breathing heavily under the moonlight. I wake him up and tell him I've got iron pills and drops, anything I could find. Blood red eyes open and he knocks my hand away. He stumbles to his feet, swinging fists like an untrained fighter.

"I don't want to do this, Tanz."

"You will die, Claremone." His voice is menacing. The dark forces have him.

He attacks, pushing me over a gravestone.

I stand and punch him in the face, knocking him out. Jumping on top of him I open his mouth and pour iron-multi drops down his throat. I collapse next to him and open the bottles, propping him up.

"Here, take these. It's not much but should help. Hopefully you're not psychotic when you come to."

I give him several pills from every container, moving his jaw up and down, hoping something will work. Some water to swallow it. Several minutes pass. He's groggy but comes to. His eyes are dark and near lifeless, but no longer red. I open more containers and give him another ten. "Dinner."

*

When I wake its morning and there's a guy mowing the lawn at the far end of the cemetery.

Tanz is still asleep.

"Can you sit up? You have to wake up, Tanz." I pull at him.

He leans forward, grabbing his head. "Ow, my head hurts."

"They'll be looking for us," I say. I don't mention punching him.

We both try standing. He stumbles, almost falling over, clutching his head as we hobble to the exit like a couple of drunks.

"I told you you'd have your opportunities…" he says, grabbing hold of me as we try to make it back out to the city limits.

*

On the street, the same group of guys I saw last night walk toward us on the sidewalk.

"We must cross."

Tanz nods, leaning on me.

They also cross.

I whisper to Tanz so he knows what's going on, "I saw these guys last night when I was getting the iron."

He looks up as they approach. "They may have been waiting for you. Can you run?" Tanz asks.

"I can barely walk," I say. "Can you touch them, or use your eyes?"

He shakes his head. "Then we must face them. Act as if you can fight." He says.

"Okay, guys, okay," he says, raising his hands.

They stop in front of us and spread out. Tanz and I take fight stances, putting up fists, but his fall. I help lift them, but they fall again then he falls onto me.

The center one with dark curly hair says, "We've been watching you two."

The one on the right, I notice, is the bicyclist. Nodding, he says, "Anyone who got set up that bad is surely no friend of Kimbel. The whole city's on alert looking for you two. Come with us. We have cars." He nods to two black Jeeps with knobby tires parked nearby.

"Who are you?" I ask.

"Friends. You must trust us… Please. There isn't much time." He motions to the Jeeps.

"We trust no one," I say. "Can you read him, Tanz?"

"My inner world is blind." His dim blue eyes radiate no light.

We look around as dark haze pop up at intersections, heading for us.

The bicyclist says, "We'd love to stay and chat but really we must get going… Are you coming?" He motions to the vehicles again; his men are getting jittery at the sight of the dark forces.

Cops blare around the corner, two, three, four cars, and race down the street at us, now only half a block away. Tanz and I hop in the rear Jeep. The haze fade as the cops arrive. The bicyclist sits in front and shouts back, "This whole town is wired with cameras and sound."

"I thought you were safe," I say.

Tanz mutters something I can't hear as he leans against the tinted window.

"We are. They aren't." The driver hits the gas and the car takes off. He points to the cops now chasing us.

"We must get beyond the city limits. Remember how fast that bicycle went? Well, I'm a mechanical engineer. So, buckle up…" As soon as he says this some booster rocket kicks in. The speedometer jumps. We careen at two hundred miles per hour climbing over cars, anything in our way, then jump over the city gates leaving the cops behind. Our heads are pinned to the backseat cushions as we fly through the air and land on the rough terrain of no man's land.

SAFETY IN NO MAN'S LAND

OUTSIDE THE CITY limits we drive for several miles through thick brush, a cover that's been tunneled through. Entering a wild area surrounded by a pack of defending wolves. The wolves escort the car while howling and yelping. They leave us at a cave entrance, the bottom of a camouflaged hillside where dense foliage grows thick enough to hide an army.

"Wolves, sir?" Tanz asks.

"Man's best friend. All it took was some training."

"You altered their DNA," Tanz accuses.

"No sir, we raised them as pups after the land was poisoned."

We park inside a wide garage with an armada of souped-up Jeeps, cars, and bicycles. We exit through a door in the rear. Inside the cave is a labyrinth of rooms and activity. The bicyclist and mechanical engineer, Mark, turns to us and says, "We'd been planning an attack before you arrived, before Kimbel turned his attention on you."

Tanz's legs buckle and he falls into my arms.

"He needs help, now! My friend is dying and needs—"

"Yes, I know, both of you need iron core crystals. We have a large stockpile. The crystals have kept us lucid and alive, not empty shells like so many. Please." We walk into a small bunker room with hard packed walls of dried mud where two soft beds lay. "Please rest. The nurse will bring in an iron crystal drip."

Mark leaves us.

I lay Tanz down and a kind woman with soft brushed hair brings in fruit and food and an intravenous drip. Tanz stops her, grabbing her hand. "What is your name?" he asks weakly.

"Belinda." She smiles.

He relaxes and lays down. She rubs his arm with alcohol on a cotton ball then pricks him with a needle, tapping the vein to begin the drip.

"You remind me of my wife," he says, smiling, then he drifts off, releasing her hand.

"Rest," she says, patting his chest. "Much to come now that you're here. It is a very good sign."

She sets me up with a drip as well. I close my eyes and sleep.

*

My eyes crack open, a man has come in to check on us. The drip bags are almost empty. Tanz's blazing blue eyes open. He stares at the man, clearly getting his strength back.

The stocky man in the white coat backs off, saying, "Whoa, you take a lot, big fella."

Tanz's eyes blare wider at him.

"That's okay, that's okay, take as much as you need. I'll bring more," the man says, backing out of the room.

Tanz and I make eye contact then fall back asleep.

EX-POLITICIAN AND REVOLUTIONARIES

AFTER A FEW days of recovery, coming to and falling back asleep, I finally wake feeling as powerful as a three-eyed glanum from the caves of Narican. A beast so powerful, it is rumored, it can lift buildings. Tanz sits up a minute later. He too is at full strength and beats his chest, smiling.

We walk down the hall outside the room and find the main hangar and operation. It's busy with people and activity. Desks, computers, multiple large surveillance monitors fill the room watching the capital for militarized movement. A man paces behind the programmers and operators.

"Greetings," Tanz declares with measured voice at the door.

Many heads swivel. The pacing man stops, turns to us, and walks closer.

"I'm glad you two are feeling stronger. You almost depleted our stockpile of crystals," he says jokingly. "I am Frank Milleron…"

"Milleron… Milleron," Tanz mutters to himself. "Senator Milleron?"

He smirks. "That was another lifetime."

"Weren't you killed or indicted?"

"Only my name, sir." He half smiles, a painful smile. "As Kimbel's power grew, he saw me as a threat and discredited me with falsehoods and innuendo. Creating fake pictures of me with another woman. My wife left me. He killed my political career with slander and lies. I owe him. But that is not why we are here, today."

Milleron is tall, with broad shoulders, big hands, and a chiseled face. Many programmers look over at him and watch. "Come, let me give you a quick tour of our facility so you can better understand your surroundings and our purpose here."

Down the hall there's a room with hanging facemasks.

"These masks are made of the iron crystals. Please take one." The room has a stockpile of the crystals on the far end.

"The cave keeps them cool, a natural refrigerant. We do our own mining of course." He points to a small drill in the center of the room.

"They don't sell this stuff on the open market as you may know. Our beloved government has kept it a secret and for themselves. We supply the black market to spread what we've learned. The sales partly fund our operation.

"Government and corporate leaders know full well that people will evolve and expand, as we have, as human beings, if the crystals spread, to finally live the way we were meant to."

The nurse walks into the room. He puts his arm around her. "My love." She's shorter than he and her soft blue eyes sparkle at him. Tanz smiles at her and nods.

"Because of this large supply we haven't given in to the fear and destruction of the planet. We will not accept that fate…" In another room with toys and projects some thirty children play.

"These are our children and our future. They receive an extra dose of inoculation to prevent a divided mind, as young ones are more easily preyed upon.

"That is how we have beaten the toxin so far. We are not afraid of the dark forces. In fact, we are here for the destiny of our souls to be fulfilled with integrity. We live opposite fear. The iron crystals have given us much insight and strength."

In the hall Tanz speaks to me telepathically. The small part of his forehead pulsates with light. Mine must be as well. I can feel my forehead warming as I cover it.

He says, *"The cleansing is wearing off faster, linking their higher DNA. Perhaps these are the news humans the council intended, the evolved ones."*

"Intriguing," he says out loud to Milleron.

Milleron leans closer to us. "Are your foreheads flashing, gentlemen?"

Tanz waves off his question and points up. "Must be the lights reflecting. Do you know where humans came from, sir?"

"God? Evolution? We are lost to that information. Irrelevant as it is. We are here now. There is a force of light that leads us. The soul that leads us is just."

Belinda and the people around him nod. He is clearly their leader.

We nod then look at each other. He introduces a few of his upper ranks standing near him. "Hancock, Bill, Bull, and well, you've met Mark and Belinda."

We nod at them.

"Now, if I may ask, who are you?"

"We are Tanz and Claremone," Tanz answers.

"That's great, now that we have your names. I'm sorry to be blunt or disrespectful, but we took great risks bringing you here, especially if you are such an enemy of Kimbel's."

I let Tanz do the talking for us. After all, he is the adult.

"We are no one special, sir. Only truth seekers ourselves…"

"We both know you are more than that, sir." Milleron steps closer, standing a foot taller than Tanz and a good fifty pounds heavier. "No human could intake that many crystals…"

"I am yet a humble accountant and he a supermarket clerk."

"That may be what you do but that is not *who* you *are*. Either way, his enemy makes you our friend and clearly you put the fear of God into him."

Tanz breaks eye contact and rubs his chin. "Please repeat what you just said, sir."

"That you put the fear of God into him?"

Tanz nods. "You have given me an inspired idea. We must act upon these. We thank you, but I must confer with the boy. Rest assured more will be revealed." Tanz turns to leave the room, taking me by the arm, then turns back to Milleron. "As we must trust your character, you must also trust ours."

As Tanz steps to leave Milleron steps closer with his commanders. "Come on, who are you two?" His voice is serious, demanding.

"Allies and friends." Tanz's eyes blaze at him and Milleron leans back. "Do you ask everything upon a friend when first meeting? We thank you for your kindness. You cannot know our identities. It is law."

Milleron's eyes bulge as he backs down. Tanz turns to leave with eyes electrified.

Milleron shouts, "I know about that device he talks on and he's not ordering pizza."

"Leave that to us. We shall return shortly."

We exit down the hall.

*

Back in our room, we sit on our respective beds. Blue pulsating equations flare off his body and disappear into the air.

"Clearly you don't need any turkey and broccoli today," I say, kidding him.

He smiles and nods. "I must find someone. Please do not interrupt."

He sits with back straight on the edge of the bed, closing his eyes. A small pulsation lights up his forehead, but he is not speaking with me.

The blue light pulsates in staccato beats, on for a few then off, as if he's receiving information as well. After a few minutes, his blazing blue eyes open. His head adjusts to me.

"We must attack."

INSANE ATTACK PLAN

BACK IN THE main room, Tanz walks over to Milleron and places his hand on his shoulder. Milleron turns. Tanz stares into his eyes with normal eyes this time. "We thank you for your hospitality. We are here to serve."

Milleron nods apprehensively, at me, then back to the monitors. "Our scanners revealed dark forces and military massing on the south rim of the city. They are planning their attack."

"Good," Tanz says.

"Good?" Milleron queries.

"We shall not meet them on the field of battle but elsewhere to better use our resources."

"Well, how are we supposed to transport our Revo fighters and equipment? We're outmanned and outgunned. Surprise was our only chance."

"Revo fighters?" I ask Hancock, the middle-aged man with thinning hair standing next to me.

He leans in and quietly says, "Revolutionary fighters."

I nod. "Ah."

"I have a plan," Tanz says.

"I thought you might. Well, what is it?"

"We attack."

"Attack? We have about two hundred well trained operatives."

"Wonderful. Plenty."

"Plenty? A frontal attack would be suicide. This guy has thousands, and serious weaponry."

"We must use efficacy and surprise."

"Right, but how are we supposed to get close to the city?" Milleron's face turns harsh. "I will not have men and women slaughtered for you."

"Nor should you, sir. Can you attack what is not in front of you? What you cannot see?"

"Please stop speaking in metaphor."

Tanz looks at me and shrugs. I nod, knowing what he needs to do. He looks at them huddled around then brings up a blue pulsating equation from his hand. It is of the topography and landscape of the area.

"There are tunnels we must get to that run under the city."

Hancock looks at the equation to see if Tanz is plugged in or how he's creating the imagery, poking his head behind and in front of him. They all seem to lean a little.

Milleron is clearly confounded by what he is seeing and what Tanz just said. "Wait. What? No. There are no tunnels under the city." But clearly he is a man who accepts what he sees.

"These tunnels were designed fifty thousand years ago by an ancient race prior to the ice age. This is all that's left of them. I have reviewed the records. They will be there." Tanz moves the equation around to focus on the hillside and where the opening should be. "Here." He points.

Bill, clean-cut, corn fed, all country, one of Milleron's highest ranking operatives, shouts, "I know that hillside, sir. Used to hunt there with the wolves."

Tanz says, "Great, you will lead us. How far out?"

"Five miles, if that, sir."

"Those are my calculation as well. These tunnels will lead us halfway to the pump stations of the capital where they are poisoning the water and air. The pump station sits under this building." Tanz points. "We will destroy the pumps that maintain this illusory bubble. We must shut this off if we are to turn people back to their soul's true intentions."

"No. That runs under the water department offices," Milleron says.

Tanz shakes his head in disagreement.

Milleron shakes his head back. "You're wrong. They were moved a few years ago and no one knew why. Perhaps this explains it."

"Are you certain?"

Milleron nods as they stare at each other.

Tanz is satisfied. He looks back at the equation and remaps its location. "This leaves us exposed once we are out of the tunnels."

"So be it!" Bill shouts again. "We'll be ready. I hate hiding anyway."

There's a murmur of agreement from the gathered men and women.

"Then we must infiltrate the State Department. That is where Kimbel is and where he kept us prisoner."

"*Infiltrate?*" one young man about my age shouts from the rear. "We don't have the firepower they do."

"Correct. Defensively we are weak. An aggressive offense is our only cogent approach. Efficacy must be demonstrated in our every movement and with that we will stand equivalent to four of their fighters. Nipping off the edges as the indigenous peoples did when outmanned and outgunned in the Everglades. Thus, forcing the Union to concede. Cunning and lies were the government's only recourse after being soundly defeated."

Reports start coming in from the programmers. "Weaponry moving in for attack, sir."

Tanz grabs his arm. "Do not attack first, Mr. Milleron. Allow them to fully commit on the south rim."

"Okay..." Milleron nods, clapping his hands together. "Prepare travel packs. We need four volunteers with shovels. Those tunnels will have thick sediment built up. Fifty thousand years' worth." He leans over to Tanz. "I hope you're right. We are risking everything."

Four young men of various ancestry step forward.

"It's going to get dangerous, gentlemen. The four of you will take the lead. You understand what that means?"

They all nod.

The kid, my age, who said we didn't have the firepower, steps up.

"It's my honor, sir, like carrying the flag. For all of us. We've been waiting for something big like this."

The other three guys who look like me nod.

Milleron says, "Boys, you make me proud."

In our room we pack in silence. It grows eerily quiet as we wait. Off in the distance the toxic barrage of shells begins falling. They're getting closer and the toxins seep into the cave's air.

We hear Milleron over the speakers: "Masks on. Red Team get to the labyrinth. The field to the hillside is half a mile long. Bomb teams launch. Open that hillside up. Help our fighters. We will be exposed.

Shovel team up front. Other teams get to the hyperjeeps." The base begins firing back from multiple locations spread over a mile to distract and confuse Kimbel's army as to our location.

A dozen of us get to the end of the cave's intricate network through tunnels of packed dirt.

"Volunteers!" Milleron extends his arm and points. "Forward."

The bombs begin striking the hillside. We give them half the distance then exit first, protected by dense forest. The day is sunny with a lone cloud floating overhead.

It's warm as the bombs' smoke rises. We jog double time as shells fall around us exploding clumps of earth. The diggers make it to the hillside and begin feverishly digging like possessed men. Sharpshooters give cover from behind us. I see no opening yet. We are exposed in the field now outside the canopy of trees and brush. Kimbel's mass weaponry are just south of our position. We are attempting to sneak around while they bomb the far edges of the Revo base.

One of the diggers falls on the right and the other three dig harder. My legs pump and I speed up ahead of everyone picking up the shovel and cause. Hancock is wounded by mortar fire. Bill stops to pick him up then keeps running for us with Hancock on his shoulder.

"Dig faster!" Milleron implores, yelling at us as they approach. "Open that up, boys. That's an order!"

I dig faster, my shovel blurring. After four feet of dirt we break through into the tunnel, stumbling in.

"Go! Go! Go!" Milleron shouts five feet away from the tunnel opening, willing the remaining group to enter safely.

Tanz makes it then stoops over, out of breath. Bill makes it, placing Hancock down.

Hancock, who must be sixty, leans against the wall, wincing. "I'll be all right. Just my leg."

Belinda the nurse tends to him, injecting and patching him up.

Milleron crouches, patting him on the shoulder. "It's not your time yet, old man."

TUNNELS

A FEW FEET in I trip over something as toxic bombs scorch the field like napalm. There's a corpse lying on each side of the entrance. Tanz walks over and crouches.

"Starved to death yet perfectly preserved. No wind in here and protected from the elements."

"Except for the ice age and hunger part," I say.

Milleron orders to, "Keep shovels at the ready."

We attach them to packs.

"Collapse the opening," he says, and Bill wedges a small stick of dynamite into the top.

We turn our backs, cover our ears, hear the pop and falling soil. Headlamps are turned on as we venture inward.

"Fifty thousand years, what an incredible find!" Milleron says, hitting the hard-packed wall. The slap echoes down the tunnel. A faint buzzing stirs as we move through the earth like worms through soil.

After a few hundred yards we turn into a wider space with tunnels connected on both ends.

"This must've been the main living area, where they slept," Hancock says. His eyes light up seeing depictions on the wall. He hobbles over to study them shining his lamp. I learn from Bill that Hancock is an ex-high school history teacher.

We follow along with him from earlier depictions of hunting with spears, bears, fire, then dancing celebrating a hunt. We follow his light to the last segment. An entity stares out with four eyes: two side to side, two up and down with an elongated forehead and scar that runs its length.

Hancock says, "He must've been their god and sits atop what appears to be a tornado." He shines his light at the ceiling and other walls. "My goodness, this is an archeological dream."

Tanz says nothing, looking away.

We keep walking and the buzzing sound grows. Down another tunnel we come upon cliffs and a stream flowing over into a dark, endless hole. Wanting to try the fresh water, I touch the stream and it burns me. Recoiling in pain, the skin on my finger sizzles.

Tanz squats and analyses it. "It is the toxin," he says, loudly, his words echoing down the chamber.

Milleron looks on. "We aren't far from the water plant. So, it may just be leaking."

The hole is twenty feet wide and the waterfall is eating a hole into Earth's core as water drops into never-ending blackness. We all look down.

"Hee hee hee… Hee hee hee." Startled, we hear this high-pitched call and increased buzzing. *"Hee hee hee… Hee hee hee."*

"What is that awful sound?" I say, covering my ears. Then hundreds of creatures fly into the open from another tunnel.

"What are those, things?" Bill asks.

We start running back to the main room.

"They look like… fanged… flying… ferrets! Yuck!" Belinda shouts covering her head.

One swoops over my head and chomps down. I duck. The fangs are twice the size of their heads. A few in the rear are chomped on and knocked into the black, toxic hole. We never hear them hit bottom. *"Ahhhhhhhh…"* We only hear their voices grow distant.

Milleron commands, "Shoot to kill! Shoot to kill!"

The gunners duck and take position.

"Hee hee hee … Hee hee hee." They swoop again, chomping with eight-inch incisors. Then, as the bullets fly, the ferrets drop.

Tanz tests one that falls near his feet. "It's as if they live off the toxin as one would food. Clearly they have survived perfectly in here, evolving and mutating without predators."

I ask, staring over the falls again, "Wouldn't this toxin eventually carve its way into Earth's core?"

Tanz nods. I shift to speak telepathically, covering my forehead with my hand as if scratching it. He does the same, but only after I clear my throat he catches on.

"Didn't you say the spirit of Narican's world was cloaked? Couldn't something similar happen here?"

"Indeed, it could," he says, rubbing his head, looking over the edge.

Deep in thought we make it to the last tunnel, which dead-ends.

"This is it, folks!" Milleron shouts. "Shovel Unit. Dig."

I unclip my shovel and start digging.

"Sir! Sir!" we hear from the rear and stop shoveling. There's a door that looks like mud yet opens into a low-lit room. The room is cold and filled with sealed metal crates.

"Those crates are filled with the toxin," Tanz says.

Flies buzz and shoot green goo that burns a hole in the guy who found the room. He gets angry then enraged, swinging at the air, then he pushes Hancock into the wall next to him. The kid's eyes turn red.

Milleron strolls over, punching the angry man hard in the face, knocking him out. Jumping on top of him, Milleron grabs serum from his jacket and injects the guy's arm. After a minute the kid comes to, rubbing his face.

"Whoa, what happened?" the kid asks.

Belinda helps him to his feet. "It's okay sweetie, you were injured," is all she says.

We back out and spray small canisters of serum into the room. The flies fall to the floor and die. Smoke rises from their quickly decomposing bodies.

We step back in looking closer at the crates.

"Tanz!" I shout. "There's strange writing on this one."

He hurries over and studies it. He leans in, rubbing dust from the crate surface, then his face goes pale.

"Tanz... Tanz... are you all right?" I shake him.

"This language," he says, staggering to his feet, "has not been used in a thousand years." His words slow. He switches to telepathy, no longer hiding the flashes. *"It was used only by a small group of tribesmen in a remote region of Rybag, Narican's third moon, just outside the universal expansion."*

"That's where Jintara's from."

A silence fills the room and the cold of it grips me tighter. The men and women stare at us.

Milleron walks up to us and says, "Come, gentlemen, we have a job to do."

Tanz says to me, "We don't have enough serum to destroy the toxin and stop the process. We must leave it." He opens the equation and drops in a few more ingredients that sparkle blue, float, and fade. "90% complete."

He checks the records again. "Nothing," he says.

Back to telepathy and covering our heads. *"What we know is whoever did this knew how to elude the universe's memory."*

"Where the universe expands, does it remember?"

"Fine question."

In the tunnel we walk to the dirt exit and hear the toxic waterfall echoing.

Milleron shouts, "Once we dig through, know your partner, form regimen lines, then double time it to the water plant. It will be two blocks from here, but two blocks above ground. Knowing Kimbel, he'll have the entire city waiting for us."

We prepare at the tunnel exit and hold off finishing the dig until we're all ready to go.

"One last thing," Milleron says. "Don't forget, *we* are the enemy…"

"Only the enemy of bullshit, sir." Bill says.

We dig for a short while then break through the hard-packed soil ending up in the crawl space of an abandoned building. Pushing up rotted wood planks that snap with ease. Piling through, we help each other out into a dusty room. There's an art easel and wood table pushed against the wall. We walk out through the white front door as if we'd just been to an art show and stopped by for a visit.

Exposed on the street we quickly form lines.

"One block straight. One block left," Milleron commands.

BATTLE FOR THE CAPITAL

Jogging past televisions with war and reality shows, the monitors switch to us and the camera zooms in on Tanz and me.

The newscaster shouts, "The murderers have escaped. There!" He points into the camera. "They're approaching the intersection of Main and South and with these cretins!" The camera zooms back out.

Milleron, up front, says to Bill next to him, "Well, that didn't last long…"

People begin filing out of buildings. They come out of stores with anger in their eyes.

"They think we killed him," I say to Tanz, disturbed by how many are filing into the street. These people look the same as the folks that came into the grocery store. Just regular folks.

We pass a cheese shop that sits across the street. The proprietor, a middle-aged man with brown hair and a short brown beard, turns his window sign to CLOSED. He walks out, wiping his hands on his white apron while carrying a large cheese knife.

The mob forms on the road slowly. Milleron mutters in disbelief, "There are so many."

"You estimated the entire city, sir. You were not wrong," Tanz states, jogging alongside me just behind Milleron and Bill. Hancock and Belinda are behind us then Revo fighters and sharpshooters carrying all sorts of weaponry.

"I'd prefer to be wrong, Mr. Tanz."

Dark forces pop out of sewer grates and swoop down from windows hovering above the growing mob. They encircle them with a dark cloud further twisting their thoughts and emotions: hatred swells in their eyes.

We make it to the intersection. "Turn here!" Milleron says.

Eight guys from Green Team meet up with us. The noise and clamor from the mob grow. Police sirens blare from a few blocks over. Sulfur is in the air.

Milleron shouts, "Nice to see you safe, gentlemen!"

Bull, the dark skinned, thick Green Team leader, agrees, "Good to be seen, Commander. First friendly faces we've seen all morning."

"And most likely your last," Tanz says. Everyone stares at him.

Bull nods in our direction. "Fun guy."

"I intended no humor. Simply stating a calculated fact."

"And an obvious one, Tanz. Thanks," I say as we continue hoofing it.

Coming around the bend there's another mob forming. It merges with the one behind us. There are hundreds on the street now and they all want our blood. No due process. No innocent before proven guilty. In front of a shop window the women in fur coats see us and glare, pulling sharp keys out of their pockets.

Monitors flash the newscaster. "They killed our leader!" he shouts into the camera. The volume increases as his words echo off buildings.

Half a block down we see the white, unmarked building that stores the pumps. The exterior has one bolted metal door on the side. There is no lobby entrance. We arrive but there's no access point.

The mob descends from up the block and fills out the street, half encircling us in a crescent shape. They're armed with sticks, rakes, tire irons: a single moving mass of vengeful seething hatred. White faces with a few scattered brown and black ones.

Standing in front of the white stucco building Revo fighters spread out to take positions shooting serum and rubber bullets into the crowd. Sharpshooters also take up positions on stoops and on top of cars.

"Take position men." Bull's team also spreads out to hold the perimeter.

The four of us stand in front trying to figure a way in. No windows. Tanz grabs a dark haze ball near his head and holds it on the lock. The gunners and trained fighters battle, struggling to keep the crowd back. The haze ball squirms, attempting to escape. Tanz squeezes harder and uses his eyes, commanding it to melt the lock as a rocket hits above us from a hoverplane exploding the door and wall leaving us standing in a cloud of white dust and rubble. A gaping entrance stands in front, exposing the massive pump station and pipes.

"Unconventional," Tanz says, flinging the dazed haze to bounce off what's left of the building. Tanz shakes his hands and arms.

Just inside sits the spray station that pumps into the water main.

"Hurry, Bill, set explosives!" Milleron shouts, pointing to the location where a section of piping comes together from the direction of the toxin.

"Yes, sir!" he says as we all duck inside. He unpacks explosives but too many bullets scream past as we take cover behind the rubble.

The military hoverplanes unleash their payload, wrecking the building but not affecting the pipes.

Bill shouts over, "They can't unload missiles, only bullets, or we'd all be dead!"

"Why?" I ask.

He nods up to the pipes and I understand.

Rocks fly from the mob and ding the metal pipes like an orchestra. Bill cannot set explosives. Too many bullets and rocks flying in. We look to Milleron for answers.

The crowd presses our fighters closer as it grows thicker with faces hostile as one's worst enemy, when within we must all want the same things.

"They won't let us!" Bill shouts to Milleron a few feet away, who's assessing the situation.

Deep in thought, he responds clearly, "We did not anticipate such hostile resistance."

On the left perimeter Hancock goes down in a barrage of military bullets. Bill shouts over, "Hancock, no!"

The fighters try to get to Hancock, but the mob swallows him whole. He's not seen again. Bill lunges forward.

Milleron stops him. "No, he's gone."

A haze cluster encircles two of our fighters. One goes insane, holding his head and running into the street then hit by a fast-moving military vehicle.

Another one climbs a building and jumps off. I lose sight of him as he's swallowed by the mob on the far side. Bull fights hand to hand.

Belinda tries inoculating who she can, but she can't inoculate from bullets or a rock to the head. She gets hit with a rock herself and our guys back her out. The mob gets hold of another two and beats them with sticks and rocks. Bull pries them out. The fighting continues while our line is breaking.

"Kimbel stripped the public of guns a few years back. Hence the rocks and sticks. Secure masks!" Milleron commands.

The cheese shop owner shouts, "They're trying to kill us by poisoning our water supply!"

Bill stands next to me scanning the growing surge. Buildings are on fire in all directions. Time is running out.

"Why won't they let us shut it off?" I say.

"Their minds are frozen in fear, distrust," Tanz says in his low measured voice.

"They've been taught the spray protects them from outsiders, man," Bill says with his rolling Midwest accent. "Don't you get it? *We're* the outsiders!"

I shout to them, "There's a drug in there. We're trying to help you!" But they can't hear above the raucous din. They wouldn't believe me anyway after the lies Kimbel has spread.

More rocks and bullets whiz at us. "They won't believe us..." I say.

Milleron turns to me with his rugged face. "Would you?"

Crouching beneath the massive structure, Tanz looks at the chaos and crumbling buildings. He speaks again with a low measured voice. "We are losing. The city is on fire. We must abandon the pump station while we can and get to the statehouse."

Once more we look at the massive pumps with twelve-inch reinforced steel and spray canister with rivets the size of my hand. We start to run. Milleron signals the group to pull out. Our gunners blaze the last rubber bullets into the crowd, slowing them. Bull and Belinda are running, too. Milleron slows down to take her hand.

Half sprinting again, Milleron speaks into his watch. "Purple and Black Teams continue with your perimeter speed assault. Dismay and confuse.

Disrupt. Spread them out, and for God's sake stay safe." He looks around the city, his city, and stops running.

We all stop to gather around him. We have a few seconds' lead. He broadcasts over his watch to the field teams, "Men and women, we do this for country, for family, for our children, the future. Justice matters that much. There are hard decisions to make. Right and wrong should not be one of them. I know this is scary. But we must win."

He then commands, shouting, "Hyperjeeps! Seven and Eight. Get us out of here. Now!"

"Be there in a second, Commander..."

The newscaster demands, "The murderers are still alive, citizens! Catch or kill them and receive five thousand capital city credits to your shop of choice!"

We start running again for the statehouse.

"I hate television. We need to shut it down and shut that jerk up!" I say then hear a whirring sound like a spaceship, *RRRRRRYYYyyyyyyyuuu.* The hyperjeeps have arrived.

*

Tanz and I hop in one with Bill. These are double-deckers in the rear with gunners at the top. We sit behind Bill and the blond driver with wavy hair is Mark the engineer. Two Revo fighters fill the upstairs seats. We go zooming off at breakneck speed. Out my window I see Milleron hit by a bullet and stumble into his hyperjeep with Belinda, Bull, and Green Team diving in behind him.

I keep it to myself while Tanz asks, "Mark, since you invented the hyper-bike, I can only assume you created this as well?" Tanz knocks on the interior materials with his knuckles.

"I sure did."

"Most impressive."

Mark shouts over the road noise and engine, "Since you're a bit of an engineer yourself, I'll tell you. The hyperjeeps are lightweight titanium for high speed ground assault and escape."

Milleron's hyperjeep turns left where we turn right. Revo fighters launch missiles at the hoverplanes. Seat belts strap firmly over both shoulders. The hyperjeep accelerates rapidly, and our heads squeeze against the headrests.

"Hang on, folks," Mark says, skidding the fat tries as we smash the corner of a building without slowing down. The digital speedometer reads: 99 mph. Who knows what it goes up to?

"First gear," Mark shouts, partly answering my question.

I nod, glancing at the gear shifter. Eight gears and the top right of the shifter says "Climb." Must be for mountains.

We bounce along streets and sidewalks flying along the ground of the city. Tanz leans over to me. "Not the best way to see landmarks. No selfie for my InstaFace page."

I nod and half smile like he's insane. He leans against the tinted window and smiles, holding up his phone and snapping pictures, trying anyway. He lowers the phone to view it. He's smiling with blurred colors behind him. He hits delete. "Not flattering." And he looks back out.

A few seconds later Tanz leans back over and says, "I'd love to drive one of these things." Which I immediately think is a terrible idea but don't tell him.

"Mark's doing just fine."

"But wouldn't you agree I'm an excellent driver?"

"Do you even have a license?"

He raises a hand at me and shakes his head. He turns, leaning forward, and asks Mark, "What does it run on?"

"Lithium and hydrogen with a hint of CO_2. It'll do four hundred, but only for short periods. Two hundred, shoot, it can do that all day." Mark points to the dash with all sorts of switches and lights. "This switch is for vertical climbs and that starts the power vacuum inside each wheel well. The vacuum inside the thick rubber tires creates reverse air flow through small pores on the tire adhering us to any surface. Wanna see?"

I shake my head, no. Tanz, of course, says, "I am quite inclined to experience this." And Mark makes a right turn onto one of the tallest buildings in the capital jamming the gear into "Climb" mode.

I hang on tight, feeling queasy. It's not for climbing mountain roads at all. I think I'm going to be sick again. These two drive exactly the same.

He then makes another ninety degree turn on what must be the fiftieth floor and we continue toward building's end. Closing in on the edge about to fly off and die when a dashboard voice speaks. "Approaching structure's end. Approaching structure's end." Instead of turning down the building toward the ground he hits another flashing button. We zoom cross across the street flying over a hoverplane that's looking for us. We land upon a shorter building, tires sucking on, then we drop diagonally across, moving fast as the ground quickly approaches, gravity pulling us. I lean onto Tanz and can't peel myself off as he leans onto the door.

The front end is going to smash into the ground. I brace my feet on the floor and hold the shoulder straps tight. That same voice says, "Approaching structure's end. Approaching structure's end. Horizontal plane. Horizontal plane." Mark hits another button and the front end lifts off like a plane landing then gradually drops its nose as the front wheels connect to the city sidewalk. He flips the vacuums off and switches back into ground gears without slowing down. Jamming it into the next one. The red digital speedometer jumps up: 180 mph!

"Oh, this stimulates me profoundly!" Tanz says, sitting up grinning like a child.

"No, Tanz, you cannot drive or hotwire this! Not by any means!" I shout at him.

He scowls, leans back, crosses his arms, and looks out the window as we hurry to the statehouse and Kimbel.

*

As the hyperjeep slows, we dive out onto the statehouse lawn. We roll as the hyperjeep blurs down the street launching another set of ground missiles at the hoverplanes coming after us. The two planes crash into buildings across the concourse.

Milleron's team is already at the meeting spot on the close side of the red brick statehouse. His arm is bandaged up. We hustle over.

Bill says, "Sir, you're wounded."

"Just a scratch. Like an old football injury."

"Sir, I didn't know you played."

"Division one champs way back when."

Bills nods in approval.

Tanz says, "Belinda, that does not appear to be just a scratch. Clearly far worse."

"He's fine, Mr. Tanz," she says, standing next to Milleron.

"I'm right here, Mr. Tanz, and quite fine."

"We meet again, huh?" I say.

"Great minds think alike," Milleron responds.

"Or get killed alike," I say.

He nods, slapping me on the back.

Milleron speaks to us all. "We have one last push in us. Our people are few but committed."

The monitors imbedded in the exterior of the statehouse sit just above our heads. They flash and the newscaster comes on speaking as if staring right at us.

"We can't get away from this guy..." Bill says, pissed off.

The newscaster points into the camera. "Citizens, they are now at our beloved statehouse! The very symbol of our country."

"Talk about Big Brother watching," Bill says, shaking his head, steadying himself for attack, peering around the corner.

The newscaster continues, "We must protect our buildings and our freedoms."

"Milleron," I ask, "where's that newscaster located? Close by, perhaps?"

He stares at me and nods. "I like your thinking, kid." He then calls out in a commanding voice, "Green Team!" Bull and his unit jog in. "Go shut him up." Milleron nods to the newscaster.

"With pleasure, sir." Bull picks three fighters and they slip off like shadows along the wall.

KIMBEL ON THE WARPATH

THE MONITORS ON the outside wall switch to Kimbel relaxing with his legs dangling over the side of his chair, watching footage of us get pummeled at the pump station. He's laughing and enjoying himself yet doesn't seem to know he's on camera. He says to someone off screen, "I do love a good fight. Especially when the odds are stacked in my favor." Then his face goes pale realizing he's on camera. He gestures with a hand in front of his throat for them to cut the feed.

The screens simultaneously switch back to the newscaster.

"It is a miracle, ladies and gentlemen. Our beloved leader is not dead. Repeat, our beloved leader is not dead." He shows a clip of Kimbel escaping from his limousine, kicking out the window.

"Having fought off the killers... he escaped. And now a dire word, citizens. Our glorious capital is under mortal attack by foreign and domestic evils. It appears that the disgraced Senator Milleron is behind this. He lies and cheats and now this, ladies and gentlemen. How low will you go, sir?" An image of us outside the statehouse flashes. The newscaster puts his hand to his ear.

"I am receiving reports that our soon to be Citizen Leader will need to wage an all-out war to protect our freedoms and that the senate should give him full powers to do so. Citizens, these are dark times indeed. Please heed this warning. Protect your loved ones. Keep them safe. And may God bless us all." A banging sound is heard in the studio. The newscaster looks off camera. The mic picks up more banging and shouting offscreen.

"Marjorie," he shouts, probably at the show's producer, "what the hell have you screwed up this time?" His eyes grow wide and his hands come up, then the screen goes blank. The outside monitors go black then quickly switch to a reality show; some brunette bimbo is chewing gum and cutting hair. "…Now this is how you create a perm."

"That's our boys. Go, Green Team!" Bill shouts. We all cheer. Refocusing on the statehouse, hoverplanes float up the streets from all directions. Numerous guard regiments march in heavy riot gear beneath them.

"Oh, shit," Bill says. "We are in serious trouble."

"I can run, Tanz. I can run real fast."

"You'll then be too weak. Your life and the entirety of the universe will be at risk."

Milleron asks in humility, "Did you just say, 'the entirety of the universe'?"

"Yes. This boy, this man he has grown into, cannot be harmed or the universe will turn to darkness. The ubiquitous suns and stars at night will go dead. However, I have an idea."

"Oh, great, I thought you might," Milleron says.

Tanz opens his jacket and pulls out his little box of strange things and searches around.

"This is nothing a little wind cannot cure." Tanz pulls out the mini-tornado and places it on the ground. His blazing blue eyes project onto it, directing it. It starts bouncing around, growing rapidly.

"Hold onto something firm…" he says as the winds pick up in a fury.

I grab the iron banister along the front entrance with Milleron and Tanz, while others grab low on the cottonwood behind us.

The troops on the lawn try to set positions but get sucked up into the vortex. The war birds teeter, wings bouncing up and down with the gusts and are knocked back, crashing into buildings blocks away. Once the sky clears Tanz squirts a hint of serum into the wind's cylindrical base. The storm wicks it up, shrinks then disappears. Blue skies return.

"We are clear to attack," Milleron shouts. "Thanks, Tanz."

I lean over to him. "You still aren't driving," I say, patting his back.

He frowns, looking away.

STATEHOUSE, KING, AND
WEIRD DEVICE

Two of the physical men-beasts come out taking up positions at the front entrance. They cross their arms like bouncers with eyes as empty as black holes. One is wearing a red t-shirt with black jeans and the other is wearing a black t-shirt with black jeans.

"I forgot about those guys," I say to Tanz.

Milleron signals the first Revo fighters to enter and fight hand to hand. They're grabbed and crushed, collapsing in a heap.

We are all in shock. Milleron sends the next wave. They keep their distance and strike hard, knocking the big men back, slashing at their legs trying to chop them down. Bill enters the fray striking one with a police baton, then lands a blow to his head. The big guy in the red shirt stumbles and throws one of the fighters against the wall.

Seeing a small opening, Milleron shouts, "You two, go! We'll take care of these guys."

We slip past the black shirted guy with Milleron behind us. He grabs an iron poker from the hall fireplace and slams it down on the guy's head, who staggers back bleeding.

"What is this guy made of?" Milleron asks while Tanz and I run down the hall.

"An empty vessel. Do not underestimate him," Tanz shouts as we look for Kimbel's office.

Halfway down we find it. My legs are thick and ready. My mind is clear. I kick the door in, and it flies off the hinges into the room taking out the other two physical guys left of Kimbell's mutated bodyguards.

Entering the room, Kimbel is on the device. Tanz says, "We must find out who's behind this."

Kimbel's jaw drops in surprise as he stands, removing his face from the screen. The sheet falling over it.

One guy in a yellow shirt gets up, tossing the door off, grimacing. Angry. Eyes squinting. The other one in green charges us from the side. I step forward quickly, kicking him three times to the head. He staggers back like a boxer.

I say, "You go for the device. I'll take care of these guys. Now's the time. Use it or lose it, right?"

Tanz nods.

With the high volume of crystals in my blood, my feet and hands start pumping fast, elevating me. I hit them hard with kick after kick. Then the punches come in a flurry. My hands shoot out striking with rapid-fire fists like a spinning pinwheel of death.

Kimbel steps out from the machine to square off with Tanz. "Why won't you submit to your new king? I am your ruler now. You must submit!"

Tanz shoots his laser blue eyes at him. Kimbel cowers. Tanz slaps him in the face. "Preventing people from aligning with their higher selves is the worst betrayal of all."

"Oh, save it. No one cares." Kimbel says then runs to exit though a side door. I zoom over with leg spinning speed and block him. He tries striking me, I duck and unload into his solar plexus knocking him back several feet. He falls to the floor gasping for air.

"You caused a lot of people pain, you asshole. Especially me…," I say. The death of my parents welling up in my thoughts. About to unload the power of the sun into his face, all the pain and twisted love I've felt, when Tanz steps in lifting him by the arm turning him to stand within inches, his eyes mesmerizing. Kimbel falls into a trance, and begins crying, stomping his feet. "I was to be a God damn king. Me! A king." He whimpers with slackened arms at his side.

"You are the damned one, never God," Tanz says.

Bill enters and The Revos take over punishing the men-beasts with martial art sidekicks and backfist strikes to the head.

"Ahh, my pets. Save, daddy." Kimbel says. But they can't reach him as another kick pounds their faces.

Bill now grabs Kimbel. "You deceived this country and it's code. This is for Hancock and all my fallen brother and sisters, you son-of-a-bitch. This is our country and it's not for sale." He strikes him so hard spit flies out of his mouth onto the screens behind him, knocking him out.

"Come, an honorable senator would love to see you." He throws Kimbel over his shoulder and nods to us as they leave the room. More Revos rush in and hold the men-beasts as my feet and hands hit them with the force of a thousand winds.

The voice on the device keeps speaking, repeating, "Have you disposed of the pariah? Kimbel?… Kimbel? Unsheathe me."

Tanz gets to the device and removes the sheet. Standing somberly for the viewer to see him yet does not speak—eyes focused, accounting. He stares in hard.

I move to the right of the monitor so I can see, but not be seen. A four-eyed entity with an elongated forehead stands on the other end in the grand palace of Narican, my home.

Tanz steps closer and says with a pissed-off tone, "I am Tanz Requiten the Seventh of the Sun Clan Council." His eyes grow wider and bluer. Waves of purity emanate into the device. "You are in violation of Soul God Order 11223 and in simpler terms, you are not the Narican king."

"You are quite wrong, Tanz the Accountant," the entity says with restraint, pointing into the monitor. "Oh, I watched your pretty wife die as a dark blade fell upon her. So sad." He pauses and speaks mockingly. "You too, boy! It was a pleasure killing that windbag of a father. No need to lurk and hide. I see everything you do and have ever done. I am your king now. You will serve me." Mr. Four-eyes steps closer. "Now that I have made your acquaintance, do you know who *I* am?" He turns his profile left then right. Cupped ears and a scar of grayish skin run along his face.

"Please, sir, enlighten us as to your identity." Tanz inquires. I step closer alongside him.

"My name is Aldana and that is all I shall say."

"Aldana?" Tanz stumbles, pausing. "Y-you cannot be," he says, stuttering, blinking, blue waves ceasing, shaking his head slowly back and forth, clearly struggling with this information. "You simply cannot be." Tanz brings up a small equation under the device. "95% complete."

I have no idea what's going on here or who this four-eyed clown Aldana is, but he murdered our families and stole our kingdom.

"Oh right, these trite little equations of yours. So, you must know this to be true, accountant. Or you are wrong."

"Of course, the equation is accurate. And yet if so, how you are Aldana? *That* is impossible." Tanz fires back.

"How is irrelevant. What is relevant is I am the king and rightful ruler here and will soon rule all the dimensions. I will blind the gods and crush your puny little world that deserves to die. All the pain it causes, the deception, lies. You have to trick people into believing." All four eyes come into focus and stare wide into the monitor.

"Prepare for attack and imminent death, and for the record, the akashic records, your beloved records, your wife will remain deceased for all eternity. I will see to that. Now prepare to join her."

Tanz studies the surroundings on the monitor with eyes rapidly taking in every detail. He straightens his back and chooses his words.

"I only prepare for life and the fulfillment of my soul's purpose."

The screen goes blank and we stand in silence. I cannot catch my breath or track a thought. A great sadness fills the space between us. We're stuck here, marooned on Earth while Narican falls into further darkness. The gods and Sun Clan at stake.

Tanz closes his eyes breathing deeply then slowly releases. "We must get to the air and end this. The dark forces of the four corners will soon be upon us. The Toxic Whisperers council will seize upon this moment."

On the wall behind Kimbel's chair the heads of commerce and world leaders watch live from monitors, perhaps determining if they will fall in line behind Kimbel's rule or whoever now takes his place. Gold name plates sit under each of the dozen monitors. The top six are of commerce, corporations, and media, while the lower six are nation leaders: New Baltic Peninsula, Ukrimia, others.

*

Outside, in a side alley The Revos and Milleron are still swinging hitting the big guy in red shirt, exhausted, from one to the next, delivering a round of punches each.

Milleron shouts over, "Nice work with Kimbel. We have him secured."

We step down onto the pavement when Bill asks, "What is this guy?"

"A physical beast. Nothing more." Tanz says.

"He has mutated genes," I shout over. Bill nods and swings again.

Tanz says to me, "We must finish this then get to Narican."

"But we don't know how to get there!"

"We will. Trust the intelligence of the universe. It guides when we are quiet and allowing." I nod trying to understand.

Milleron throws one last exhausted punch and is bleeding again as his stitches have opened. Belinda stands off to the side watching. A Revo fighter throws a side kick that knocks red shirt flying into the garbage cans. We leave him there.

Walking down the alley, Tanz says, "We must be swift in our attack knowing who's behind this." He pauses and brings up his equation sprinkling in a few more facts. I anticipate it will move to one hundred percent, but it does not budge from 95% Complete, before it evaporates.

"How can that be?" I shout in frustration, wanting this to end.

"Facts are missing. The equation is infallible. Be patient. More will be revealed." He pats my back. "As always, the closer you get to truth, the more that truth desires to be known. Universal law. We must get to an airship. The dark forces of the Toxic Whisperers will soon fill the sky." We walk out in front of the statehouse and stop. Belinda tends to Milleron.

"You knew that four-eyed man?" I ask.

"I knew of him…"

"Well, are you going to tell me who he is?"

"A ghost really. His name is Aldana and well, he was your mother's much older half-brother."

"My mother didn't have any brothers."

"He was cast out of the dimension long before you were born. Indeed, long before I or your mother were born." He shows images and events of the time. "The Toxic Whisperers and Sun Clan had a brief truce eons ago that created Aldana as a peace offering to both sides. Soon he was rebellious and angry and never felt pure on either side… as he was not… Though both sides tried to comfort him, he was resentful, feeling more a byproduct than an act of love. He had no true home. His young head swelled with destructive rage, attacking Narican and murdering Chenoro of the Whisperers dark council, who he accused of being soft and weak, yet had brokered the tentative peace deal. They had no choice but to remove Aldana, cast him out so as not to tear apart the universal thread."

"So what became of him?"

Tanz shakes his head. "Rumors. Innuendo. The records show nothing. He disappeared. A ghost, as I said. But he is here and clearly seeks revenge. It is also clear which side of his soul he chose."

Belinda, Bill and the Revo fighters break off on Milleron's command. The three of us jog in silence toward the airfield where ships and hoverplanes rise to patrol the city looking for us.

CHOPPER AND TANZ FLYING

We sneak onto the airstrip through a hole in a chain-link fence. Most of the troops are on the ground in the city searching for us. We get to the crazy looking chopper, half-submarine and half-ball with chopper blades on each side built into the wings.

Standing at the base of one near the door, I ask, "Can you fly this thing?"

"Not yet..." Tanz says, he smiles, eyes growing wide, overjoyed. "Since you wouldn't let me drive that hyperjeep..." He brings up the schematics and hotwires the chopper, popping off a panel near the front.

I roll my eyes, knowing what I've gotten myself into.

Milleron stands in shock, not fully registering what Tanz is doing. "Nothing should surprise me about you two."

The entry door comes down. Tanz goes in first. "Time is of the essence, sir. Please board."

"He's a bit of a thief in case you hadn't noticed," I say to Milleron as we head up the ramp.

I hear from up front. "Necessa—"

"Yes, yes, necessary means. Let's roll, Accountant," I say as we find our seats and strap in.

Tanz punches a few buttons and the massive gunship rises above the city.

"We'll be arrested or killed. Shot out of the sky!" Milleron shouts, holding on as Tanz moves the thruster forward.

We hear over the radio, "Airship 431 out of Field Eleven, illegal launch. Illegal launch." We see #431 imprinted on the dashboard.

Once we rise above the buildings, smaller and same style airships turn in pursuit. They close in from the city sectors like a midair gang. Orders to blow us up come over the radio.

"Not today. Not for Anselier," Tanz says jamming the thruster, making calculations, and turning knobs.

"Who's that?" I ask.

"My wife," Tanz says, outmaneuvering the first wave by dropping down.

Gunships come at us from the side and rear. Tanz drops the nose further toward the street, flying into tunnels in the speed pass lane, smashing through tollbooths.

"Never cared for them." Tanz says. Milleron raises an eyebrow, holding on.

Up and around buildings, doing crazy zigzag stunts over the congested roadway.

Milleron says, "I think I'm gonna be sick."

I lean over to him in the rear seat. "That's how I usually feel when he drives."

Several ships close in on us and launch missiles, hitting our hull. There's damage underneath to the rear. The right wing is smoking. The navigation, radio, and dash lights go out. Red warning lights flash on the dash.

Milleron shouts, "How the hell are you going to fly this bird? We're blind. Need to abandon ship! Get us out of here." We're smoking and losing power.

Tanz brings up a calculation and his own pulsating blue radar and navigation map, placing them on the dash. Milleron stares like he wants to say something but doesn't know what.

"We can't get a good shot at the pump station being chased like this. Must ditch enemy birds at once," Tanz says, flying lower over the streets, angry mobs everywhere, fists in the air.

"That's why we're flying to avoid them and to end this false reality. Deception is intolerable. Anything that distorts truths," he says, swerving around a ship tail in front of us."

"We must save them, yet they want us dead, Tanz," I respond.

"Only their ignorance and hatred do."

"You do know we're being chased by the best trained pilots in the world, right?" Milleron shouts at him.

"As you may have surmised, sir, I am not from this world," he says, smiling, then he dives lower, skipping off the ground doing half a loop around other planes, cutting back the thrusters and hitting the brakes. Upside down we come crashing onto the top of an airship, knocking him out of the sky. Tanz is playing chicken, bumper cars as missiles whiz by striking buildings.

"The city's getting blown up."

He nods, understanding this battle has to stop.

"He's a bit of a cowboy," I shout to Milleron behind us. He's holding his stomach while we both hold on for dear life.

Tanz straightens the bird, slowing it, waiting for warbirds to come up the rear then twists our ship flipping out the tail and smacking them into buildings like a pit maneuver cops use, knocking out the rear of cars. I learned it in a video game.

"Order 11223, what was that?" I ask.

He shrugs and shakes his head. "Don't know," he says, focusing on flying.

"You bluffed?"

"Made it up. I only account for victories and the fulfillment of one's purpose. Nothing else is worth focusing upon." He dips and shoots a tactical shot at the ship behind us, hitting them, jamming their propellers but low enough so they can land safely. "Enough child's play," he says out loud to them as we fly low over the streets to the pump station.

A few more airships come in. Tanz makes minor modifications and the plane goes even faster, taking off. *"GGGGgggggggg FFFFfffooorrrceee,"* he yells with spittle across his face. Airships fall back as he blazes fast forward, rising and sinking, assessing, accounting, calculating. My head is pressed against the seat like a ride at the fair. My head bounces. I can't lift it.

We loop around the city perimeter shaking any remaining guys who fall away. Several crash, not able to keep up as Tanz flies full speed around the capital, swinging out to no man's land. Loop after loop after loop. I close my eyes.

"Now, first things first, the water plant…" He slows the bird pulling up front, cutting all but the hover engines. Milleron and I try to breathe normally again. We sit approximately twenty feet above the street and fifty from the building.

"You know you're blowing up their water supply, right, Mr. Tanz?"

Milleron asks, concerned as the mob grows below, funneling in from streets, holding their fists up and throwing rocks that ding against the ship.

Tanz nods, turning the nose of the plane vertical, and shoots the base of a huge satellite dish that sits atop a building. As it comes down everyone flees below. It crashes to the ground in front of us resting like an enormous metal bowl.

The mob with red murder in their eyes throws rocks and sticks at our hovering craft, anything they can hurl.

"Hit that button, Claremone. Hit it now!"

I launch missiles. We hit what's left of the white stucco building then rip into the pipes and pumps. The mob scatters for safety.

A toxic plume goes up. The permanent false yellow sun around the capital fades and that dark cloud is visible for the first time. Rain begins to fall. The dish fills with water before Tanz flies off.

DESTROY TO LIVE

WITH PEOPLE EVERYWHERE on the street, we fly low over the scattered, disoriented mob. "They'd kill us if they could," I say.

"They're just confused," Milleron responds. "They're good people and mean well. We can't give up on them." He shakes his head, looking out. "Well, some of them."

Tanz slows the aircraft so Milleron and I can hear him clearly. We stop flying to hover in a quiet industrial area out of sight behind rusting warehouses.

"Our strikes must be tactical: crucial buildings and operations only," Tanz says. "The dark forces are coming, and time is limited. We must blow up the statehouse and the entire infrastructure before they arrive."

"No that's ridiculous!" Milleron replies. "You can't. I disagree."

"We must. Nothing will change if we do not. The dark forces will overrun the land and simply replace Kimbel. This will at least give people a fighting chance to start anew."

"I firmly disagree, Mr. Tanz. That statehouse is the very symbol of our country's ideals."

"Ideals live within us, sir, and are passed down." He shows images of fathers and mothers teaching their children, showing them right from wrong.

"Kimbel wants to be Earth's king," I say to Milleron.

"What? That's impossible. This is a democracy."

"That's what I told him," I say.

Tanz continues, "If successful, he or someone else will rule Earth while Aldana's dark forces remain his ally—until they no longer find him useful."

Milleron goes quiet.

Tanz concludes, "World leaders watch from monitors in Kimbel's office. They are waiting to see if they will become subjugated partners."

"Wow, that guy is out of his mind..." Milleron says, looking out the window.

"Not so at all. Simply opportunistic, aligned with his belief system and soul's purpose. People will never believe us, or our intentions. And they do not need to. They must find it in themselves. Their minds are currently too entangled to trust us. We must take out the men in the shadows, the string pullers, and give the human race a chance. Sometimes you must destroy something to let it live. Wouldn't you agree, Senator Milleron? Is that not what happened to you?"

Milleron nods slightly. "Okay."

"We will set course for the statehouse." Tanz turns the knobs, we begin moving slowly above the warehouse's gravel parking lot.

Tanz and I look at Milleron, who seems to get a second wind, nodding more confidently. "Let's do this. Change is in the air," he says.

"We'll first hit commerce then the statehouse to disrupt all operations." The rain falls harder, and gray clouds enclose the city. The black matte sky is gone and only thunderclouds remain.

We fly several blocks across the city then shoot tactical missiles at the tan commerce building. It crumbles and all of its lies with it. Two blocks over we take out the red statehouse. A cloud of dust and debris billows.

We watch the red statehouse crumble. Milleron has tears in his eyes.

"I am sorry," Tanz utters to him. "But what good is a symbol if it no longer holds true?"

Milleron nods rubbing his eyes. "We will rebuild and write laws that preserve our ideals. And never let them slip away again."

As we fly back through the city people are dropping their rocks and sticks. They look around as if coming out of some daze as the rain falls upon them. Hatred gone from their eyes. One little girl hops in puddles. Many people walk with cupped hands tasting the sweet rain.

Milleron breathes deeply, looking out the window at the remaining city.

He speaks into his watch, "All teams, meet at the rendezvous point."

GOODBYES WITH THE
ADVANCED HUMANS

JUST OUTSIDE THE city limits, the nurse and a few other Revos come out from the perimeter and walk toward us. The wolves gather at the edge of the forest. Milleron and Belinda hug and kiss. He stares, smiling at her. She smiles back with devotion. He drops to one knee and reaches out his hand, taking hers in his.

"Belinda, I've loved you forever. Will you start a new world with me?" She nods, smiling back. "Will you marry me?" he asks.

She smiles down upon him. "Why yes, I will, Senator. Yes, I will." She bends to kiss him then also gets down on one knee in a long passionate embrace. As the world crumbles, their love has grown stronger.

The hyperjeeps pull around and the drivers, Mark included, stand at their vehicles. The wolves howl seeing their family safe again. Milleron and Belinda and the Revos all laugh.

"It has been a pleasure to meet you all." Tanz puts out his hand for Milleron to shake. "Congratulations." He nods to her as well. "I am happy for you both. We must put our plan into action now. The dark forces will attempt to consume all sentient beings on this planet. We will not let them."

Milleron says with his arm around Belinda, "Please call on us if you are ever in need."

"We most certainly will." Tanz says.

I shake their hands as well. Tanz hugs her.

Milleron says, "I didn't know we had such friends in high places."

"You shall build your home in accordance with your soul's true purpose.

The gods will be watching. So will we. That was the ideal of this nation and that statehouse. You will build another with laws to ensure that."

"We will, Mr. Tanz. We will."

"Lastly, you must help others find their truths."

"You have our word."

"Do you know who we are now?"

He smiles and laughs. "I know enough."

"Come, we'll give you a lift back to the base," Tanz offers, wanting to fly the airship once more.

Milleron raises an eyebrow placing a hand over his stomach. We shake our heads *No* at him.

"I promise, it will be a pleasure cruise… Belinda, madam? Please."

We board and fly leisurely back to their camouflaged home. The wolves follow along the hyperjeeps below.

Inside the hangar the guards march Kimbel out.

"Now what should we do with our captive here?" Milleron wonders.

"I have rights," Kimbel demands with his hands cuffed behind him.

"No longer. Treason is what you have."

"Milleron, I have a symbolic and fitting idea." Tanz leans in, whispering to him.

Milleron laughs emphatically. "Perfect, Mr. Tanz."

We bring him into a room. Tanz sets calculations and Belinda administers an I.V. The liquid is murky. "His sentence shall be what it deserves to be," Tanz says. "Though most crimes do not warrant DNA tampering, in this case… it is fitting…"

"By your actions you have chosen your own fate, you piece of crap, Kimbel." Milleron says then punches him in the face. "That's for what you did to me. And this is for what you did to my country." He punches him in the gut dropping him to floor.

Belinda turns on the drip and after a few minutes his color changes turning gray, growing fur, and he shrinks down becoming a rat who scurries to the wall looking for escape. Milleron catches him and places him in a cage.

"What will you name him?" I ask.

He thinks for a moment.

"King."

SATELLITES

AFTER OUR GOODBYES, Tanz and I get into the airship and fly back inside the city limits.

"Where are we going? I thought we needed to get home and prepare," I ask as we land in front of the capital's power grid. "Tanz, the dark forces are coming! We need to prepare, remember?"

"One thing at a time." We park and step outside of the ship. "You said earlier that we needed to shut off the televisions."

"Yeah, so?"

"Well, that's what we are doing." He connects in using his phone. Numbers begin running across the screen. "My God, whoever set this up was an imbecile. I cannot factor what an imbecile does for there is no pattern." He pauses, frowning.

"Well, shut the whole thing off," I say, looking over his shoulder.

He shrugs. "Maintenance," he says then smiles. "Reconfiguring." He looks up to the sky then checks the numbers on his phone. "It will take them some time to override this."

"What did you do?"

"Oh, nothing really, maneuvered a few satellites." He shows images of satellite arms and mirrors turning and reflecting different angles, antennas shifting. Several satellites crash into each other.

"Unnecessary means," he says.

"Quite unnecessary," I say.

City monitors switch to comedy shows and laughter, nature shows, bird documentaries. We watch the closest one playing sports bloopers as an outfielder runs into center field wall then falls making the catch.

"Now that's what I call entertainment," Tanz says.

We hop into the airship to get ready for Aldana's forces.

SPIRIT END

HEADING BACK TO Big City we park the ship in no man's land and hoof it across the train bridge. The city is thick with troops and armored vehicles.

A man and woman stride past speaking lively. "The state building was just blown up and Kimbel's missing," the man says to the woman. "It's war, but with who?"

Tanz looks at me.

Downtown in the business district armored cars are parked on street corners in front of financial buildings. Soldiers with machine guns stand protecting them.

We're looking for the spirit lady and find her tending to a grieving elderly man who's feeding pigeons two blocks down.

We stop a few feet away. Tanz's forehead pulsates. He covers it with his hand as if scratching it and speaks with the spirit lady who smiles at us. She ponders his statement while looking up at the sky. She nods upwards then pauses, as if speaking to someone above her. She then nods at us and smiles continuing with her task of tending to the grieving man who blows his nose and sighs.

Tanz says to me, "All is ready. You know what to do, right?"

I nod. We walk around the corner into an alley and I start pedaling my feet, slowly hovering in the air above him. Garbage bags swirl underneath me. "Wish me luck," I say.

"You do not need luck. But good luck just the same." He watches me proudly like a father would.

I pedal faster and faster, shooting up above city skyscrapers through cloud cover to where the atmosphere thins just before space to meet the dark forces. Out alone patrolling the edge, I hear Tanz's voice. *"Be careful up there. They will be dangerous. Do not give in to dark temptations."*

"I'm ready for anything," I say, feeling my forehead pulsate, seeing the light above my eyes. I drift outside of orbit and the interception point to witness the universe. Tanz is using me as bait once again.

While I wait, incredible stars and constellations captivate me, like seeing the universe for the first time. More stars by the billions than I have ever seen camping. I wait for the dark forces and look around. The silence is as haunting as the beauty is amazing. Yet I am so alone out here illuminated by stars from a million miles away. I want to lay back like on a grass field in the summer and watch. No fireflies are out here. Maybe the dark forces won't come at all. But I know better and look around. Nothing.

After naming a few star clusters and constellations, what I can remember from astronomy class, I cross hands behind my head and float further out of orbit pedaling occasionally to adjust position. Still no dark forces.

As I settle in from left to right stars begin fading. Dropping my hands bolting upright seeing a black hole swallowing up space. It's like a storm blowing in. I drift out to investigate, look down and the Earth is gone. My bearings are gone. While light is being swallowed up.

I get ready for a fight. But against what? Peering into the darkness, it's soundless as it moves through the particle-less void. My brain is slow to process, with no smells, no sound, and fading light.

Disoriented by the darkness, my feet spin slower. None of my senses work in the emptiness of space. I spin looking in all direction, up and down, making myself dizzier. My pedaling slows to a stop…I still see nothing but blackness, feeling lightheaded and cold.

Is this the dark forces? If so, I don't know what I'm supposed to do. I was expecting to see entities. That was the plan.

I call to Tanz. *"I need help. I can't see—Tanz are you there?"* No response. My forehead is not illuminating. Growing faint and unclear I shake my head as the rest of the stars fade.

"Tanz if it's them I don't know what to do. I can't see. Help."

I feel physical pressure on my lungs and body pressing in. My head aches, my skull is hurting.

I rotate again feeling something slimy touch me like swimming in a grassy lake. I flinch tucking my legs up but can't see into the darkness. I spin again feeling weaker, colder, disoriented.

A small yellow light appears. *"You must move. Now! They are upon you."* Syol the trainer floats in front of me, meditating upon a lavender lake under onyx mountains. His yellow third eye stares.

"Something is clouding me," I say.

"You are being swallowed alive."

This jars my thoughts as the pressure builds.

"Move to where? I can't see."

"Run! Now!" His image fades into darkness.

I pedal hard zipping forward in what direction I do not know, just moving. Pumping my legs. The coldness increases. The pressure becomes unbearable like I'm running inside concrete trying to break free.

Pedaling hard and blind, the pressure squeezes my body tighter, I can barely move—my—legs. Pumping—pumping—pumping hard. Feeling sluggish. Having trouble raising my knees… Must—keep—pedaling. Gritting my teeth, grunting, groaning. For Sun Clan, for friends, for light, I—keep—pedaling. Don't know if I'm heading into a monster's mouth or what.

I have one last push when my legs almost fly off my body, tension released. Stars are seen again. Earth comes into view far off on my side. I'm closer to Mars and turn zipping toward Earth and the protective shores of the atmosphere to defend it.

I hear Syol's voice. *"Stay within earth's orbit. You are protected there."*

Within Earth's orbit, I begin smelling again, hearing. Satellites float past. I hear their transmissions and beeps, adjusting mirror and arms.

Slowing up, realizing how hard I'm breathing with a stinging pain in my chest like some giant kid sat on me. I almost lost my life orbiting downward pedaling slower as I descend. Gravity pulls at me and I let it.

Half the globe away from where I was supposed to intercept the dark forces, I pedal down to what looks one of the snow peaked Himalayas. I stop pedaling, and glide down to rest for a moment to catch my breath and calm myself, trying not to dwell on what just happened. I breathe deeply for several moments, breathing in the cold crisp air, regaining clarity and composure, calming. The stress and confusion fades.

I connect to the metamorphic rock, snowpack and pine trees below. As they are fulfilling their purpose, I must fulfill mine, placing my hands down to push off and fight the dark forces, my forehead pulsates.

"Claremone? Claremone? Please respond. Can you hear me?"

I smile hearing Tanz's voice. *"I've never been so glad to hear you before."*

"What has happened? We lost transmission."

"There was a storm. I was watching the stars and—"

"There are no storms in space. It is them."

"Well, I know that now. It was like a black hole sucking up all the light. It caught me by surprise."

"Interesting," he says pausing. *"Where are you now?"*

"I'm safe. Just getting some air. But they are coming."

"Do not allow your light to be transmuted by darkness."

Feeling better, I smirk staring down the steep decline. *"Is this your way of saying, you miss me?"*

"Stay within earth's atmosphere. It will protect you from the harsh climate of space like a rocky cove protects from the harsh winds at sea."

I nod understanding what he means.

"Additionally, Aldana's dark forces cannot remain a miasma of electromagnetic impulse. They must adhere to earth's properties. The atmosphere will not allow them to remain en masse. They must separate into individual entities here."

"I got ya, Tanzy."

There's a pause. He must be annoyed, or we lost transmission again.

"The name is Tanz. However, as a boy, I always did seek a nickname. Tanzy will be fine, if that's the best you can come up with."

I smile taking one final look around then zoom back up getting into position, a little ticked they almost got me. I have friends I want to protect.

*

I reenter the atmosphere and see forms exiting the dark portal filling the horizon like an invading army.

"I, I can't believe how many—"

"Stay Focused," Tanz says.

The first ones out take position up front. They must be the baddest nasties they've got. Others pour out like wasps behind them.

"How can so many travel inside a black hole?" I ask backpedaling, shocked at their sheer numbers. Controlling the elements, I remind myself, remembering the tornado and black matte sky.

"Another dimension has sent them here." Tanz says.

Out here alone, I shake my thoughts clear, nod and move. If they catch me or touch me, I will become drained, disoriented, lost, as Tanz put it.

In the space outside the atmosphere I couldn't hear them. But sound moves through substance, that I know. Energy moves through waves. Inside the atmosphere and coming from the portal I hear screaming, skin curdling, jumping off the dust particles—like pigs squealing at a slaughterhouse.

I need to commit and get close to them, but don't want to. I pedal in and see their ugly details. Smelling my blood, their heads snap in my direction like hound dogs.

"You would be a prize catch." Tanz reminds me.

"Thanks, Tanz."

"Anytime."

The portal sits just outside of the atmosphere. They all look different like from different places: the four corners.

I pedal holding my position studying them, letting them see me, smell me as instructed, letting their hunger grow from half a football field away. A satellite passes close by and the stars twinkle beyond. But I'm out here alone on the edge.

Wicked faces and witches from other worlds, evil and sinister fill the sky.

The one out front is fierce and stops to look around. He must be the leader. Bones stick out from the perimeter of his face like his face is in prison. He has a head and torso with wings, and what looks like attached organs floating beneath him, pumping. Though I'm not sure if it's a him at all. His crooked red face half smirks sizing me up as I pedal maintaining the short distance. He reviews his troops then looks to the portal as more pour through.

An ugly thing behind him has a chunk missing from his head, one eyelid and half his forehead are gone, gray decomposing skin with bugs crawl on it.

On the other side of Prisonface in triangle formation is the opposite, a thin creature that looks like it was squashed by a truck. He wears a tattered blue cape. One arms glows like a log in a fire. His eyes also glow red with flame.

Hordes of wicked faces, witches, and other ugly ass dark forces behind them take up position like an army across a field. All focused on me waiting for orders.

Gulp. So much rides on this.

Boneface signals attack. His organs move forward like a rudder on a ship pointing straight at me.

His wings flap and bones extend from the perimeter of his face, twenty, thirty feet, and more. They extend out rapidly. The attack is quicker than I expected. I backpedal surprised by the attack. Not enough time to turn as they're all unleashed. His neck and face extend inside the bone prison a few feet behind the sharp tips. Witches swing out to the flanks expanding up and down in elevation filling the space. And his lieutenants are close by on his flanks.

The spear tip bones are on me in hurry and his chopping teeth right behind them. Turning and startled, I kick a few bones away that bend out then snap back into place. His neck snaps back into his torso and he scowls.

His first lieutenants come around. Buggy Chunkhead on my left and Firearm on my right. Witches swoop wanting my head and would rise in rank if they got it.

"Brrn, dada, brrn, dada, fss, fss. Brrn, dada, brrn, dada, fss, fss." I hear them speaking in tongues, languages from other worlds.

As Chunkhead approaches bugs fly out of his skull at me like a squadron.

Several satellites pass us in orbit. I dart closer for cover trying to outmaneuver them as the mirror arms turn and splat. It's like a giant fly swatter in space.

Distracted by Chunkhead, Firearm hits me; my skin sizzles. The witches swarm trying to draw out my blood, encircling me while speaking to each other. I kick a few to escape. But they stay close on my tail as Buggy and Firearm fall back.

I shout through my forehead looking left, right, up and down. *"There are too many and they're too fast! I need to get out of here."*

"Stay focused."

"I can't keep them off me," I look right then left.

"Brrn, dada, brrn, dada, fss, fss. Brrn, dada, brrn, dada, fss, fss."

"They must fully commit to the atmosphere. Not energy projections within the portal. The portal must be emptied."

We fly around in orbit, fighting. As we come around, more filter through the portal, but the numbers are thinning.

A witch with a gnarled face and stubby horns sinks teeth into my ankle. Gnaws on me. Another seems to be working on some spell, conjuring something up to put me in as a small prism appears.

With its teeth in me, hatred pours into my mind like a storm. Images of myself with horns, jagged teeth, anger, raging at life.

My mind grows cloudy. A battle rages within me.

"Tanz I can't hold—" I shake my foot struggling to get her off as we go around orbit again. Another strikes me in the neck. I'm trying to stay conscious.

All the ugliness of life, hardships, heartbreak. I see their pain. Understand them. I am just like them. Ghastly faces that look like the ones from my closet: scratchy hissing voices, horned creatures. They *are* my family. No wonder they called to me. I slow my pedaling and smile at them like a homecoming.

But wait, something's wrong. Smell. Something smells horribly wrong like rotting eggs. My minds snaps awake. My eyes focus. Witches breath on me with rancid hot breath. I lower my legs and straighten my back. The prism grows larger between them. They surround me as the prism approaches. The stench gets worse.

I dry heave and drop in elevation. Spinning into a backflip I kick one in the head and throw another into the prism that sparkles like black diamonds then is gone.

Pedaling hard to get away, I shout, "Don't you ever shower or brush your teeth?" They come after me harder. I don't know if the smell is a weapon, but it sure works like one. And not a bar of soap among them!

I get a few feet away when Prisonface and Buggy return for more. Ugly bastards. Organs drag below trying to wrap around my legs like a jellyfish. Up ahead I see the atmosphere's edge. The witches coming back around trying to corral me into space getting on both sides and under me, driving me toward the void. As we orbit, I see the hordes waiting in formation below.

I keep a few feet away outmaneuvering Buggy and a witch trying to corner me.

"You must wait for them to fully commit." He is really getting on my nerves. I nod, heading around Earth again.

"Keep moving. Do not stop."

The portal is emptying. *"Almost there."* I go around with them on my heels. The hordes wait a mile or two beneath us.

"One more pass and it should be empty." We move around orbit when a witch strikes my thigh from the side that feels like a bee sting. Instant sadness slows me.

I shake my head coming around orbit again and see the thinning numbers emptying into our atmosphere as the cloud in my mind grows.

Three exit the portal, then two, then one. I backpedal waiting for more. Nothing.

I shake off the sadness, dissolving it with light. Feeling stronger. Feeling the light of Narican. I throw one ugly into space. It is crushed by the pressure and dies. A spinning back kick into another while my fists unleash a turbine into the face of another sending it to spear onto the antenna of a fast-moving satellite.

As the portal is emptied, Prisonface and the others turn away from me to take up position in front of the hordes. Preparing to descend they turn toward Earth.

I drop down to watch. The dark forces stretch around the globe miles above the cloud cover. They're hungry for humans, easy prey as Tanz once put it. And the humans are unaware of what's coming for them as they raise kids, work jobs. The dark forces want to enslave them.

Prisonface takes one last look at me hovering above then turns away. His organs signal to descend. The hordes follow.

"No, stop," I shout burning along in front of them. They ignore me.

"Brrn, dada, brrn, dada, fss, fss. Brrn, dada, brrn, dada, fss, fss."

Quietly chanting, smacking lips. Grunting and howling as if coyote's about to feast. I dart through them, but no resistance. Like diving through a wave trying to move the ocean. They ignore me.

I float off to watch confirming their commitment. The black hole above waits silently. I place hands on the sides of my head, fingertips over my temples.

"Okay now! They're coming," I send out through my forehead, feeling the words sprinkle down to earth.

*

I slow my pace to watch not sure what's going to happen. Light rises in a wide band like a gamma ray cannon exploding from Earth's surface. Brilliant colors burst up like fireworks.

The woman spirit and thousands of other spirits rise. Flowing silhouette forms and shimmering auras illuminate the lower atmosphere with golds, silvers, aqua-blues, oranges, pinks. They're smiling, holding hands, radiating love as they rise.

The descending dark forces howl and squeal in ecstasy seeing them approach.

Both seeing the value of the human soul.

Prisonface's bones extend out as the two sides mover closer to colliding.

Firearm rotates his shoulders, loosening up like a baseball pitcher. Buggy Chunkhead's bugs swirl around his head like a moving halo. The witches begin to conjure—the decrepit hordes follow.

I can only watch. *"Who are these spirits? Why did they choose this?"* I ask Tanz, realizing how worried I am about them.

"Love is their fate. Their commitment," Tanz says.

"But who are they?"

"Pure love unexpressed when in physical form."

"They were alive once?"

"Very much so."

I nod, pondering this, watching, worrying, trying to understand.

Tanz continues, *"At death all sentient beings return to pure form."*

"They're from Earth?" My anxiety increases learning this as the two sides close in.

"Some, I surmise. Could be multiple places they have visited during their journeys. Such as yourself." This comment triggers memories of my past life on Narican and the dark forces that killed my family. Some may be here now among this group.

The howling frenzy increases as the spirits approach and dark forces descend.

"But what will happen when they impact?"

Tanz calculates. *"The outcome is uncertain."*

I pedal more, wanting to help, but Tanz reminds me, *"There are powers beyond us…"*

About to hit, the spirits glow brighter and light expands. A raucous rumbling erupts from the descending band like a heavy metal concert. Shrieking and screaming, grunting and growling, horns and fangs—scary nightmare beings seeking carnage.

As they impact and swirl the light dims then becomes brighter, stronger, then dims again. At first, I can't tell who's winning within the swirling, churning winds. But with wave after wave of the dark forces, their sheer volume outnumbers the band of light beings. As the black cloud swirls the light diminishes as if being gnawed upon by a school of piranha. Witches diving in. The frenzy and volume increases—awful squealing and high pitch yelping pierces the air.

"Nooo, Tanz!"

"What is happening?"

"They're dying. The light, it's going out… I can't stop it…" I pedal closer to the spinning winds fighting against the undertow.

"The spirit light is fading, disappearing. Oh God, what have we done?"

I travel around the globe to see.

Over the Alps, the peaks are in darkness as the darkness travels down the mountains' bases. Darkness spreads across the Earth like an eclipse.

I pedal more, harder. Darkness passes over the artic glaciers.

I zip farther and faster. It passes over atolls in the Atlantic.

I pedal in a fury now lower to the surface. The ocean waters part beneath me like the wake from a cigarette boat.

I pedal to Big City where building tops are enshrouded in dense toxic clouds.

People fight in the streets.

I keep spinning my legs harder, faster, confused, angry, distraught.

I complete the globe and slow my pace as the thick cloud now encircles the Earth. Though late afternoon daylight turns to heavy dusk.

The grunting and growling quiets. The howling mutes. Clearly the darkness has won—nothing left to feed upon.

The light and spirits are gone as the swirling black and gray cloud continues spinning and churning. The rusty sun struggles to penetrate.

The humans are next. But what can I do? They are no match for the dark forces. And neither am I.

The thunderous rumbling quiets. There is silence in the darkness: pain, confusion, and silence. Just like on Narican, I couldn't save my family. Just like here, I couldn't save my parents. And now this. What good am I or the light beings if we can't save anyone?

I pedal slower now, unsure what to do. Empty and lost.

"Tanz, I feel sick." But he doesn't respond.

I pedal slower, lowering into the southwestern desert to sit upon red rocks and catch my breath.

Sitting at the top of a butte I try breathing deep, but it doesn't help. Too disconnected, sad. I drop my head into my hands, feeling weak, having failed again.

What's the stupid point of it all?

I wonder if my friends are all right. I should probably just stay here and hide. I look around at the beauty of the red rocks, stark and intense. I could camp, live off the land.

But feeling sorry for myself won't bring the spirits back. And I have friends who need my help. I take another deep breath letting it out slowly. I rock my head back and open my eyes breathing in the clean desert air. Dragging myself up to stand about to pedal off to Big City when up above buried in the clouds I see a faint light…

Then it's gone…

Nothing but gray and black from other worlds fill the space.

I scan the sky, hoping. Nothing.

Then I see it ever so faint again. Then nothing.

It might just be an airplane but a tiny orange light blinks inside the cloud.

I realize I don't hear any airplanes. I listen harder, cupping my ear.

Wait, there it is again and in the same place. It can't be an airplane! This time it lasts a second longer. I drop down from the rock and begin jogging along the red dusty soil in its direction. It better not be an airplane.

I scan the sky… Is the light flickering or blinking? Now a green light pops up near it. I jog faster along the trail past prickly pear cactus.

I pedal up into the sky to get a closer look. Both lights flicker, expanding a few inches in diameter, then stop.

Holy crap! I pedal out to the ocean where a red light glows inside the thick gray cloud. Farther out a purple circle hangs over the islands like a dim lamp.

As I get closer this purple light grows into a band of light that penetrates down to the ocean surface like a spotlight at the circus.

As I keep going thin streams of blue cut through the cloud like a waterfall illuminating a pod of swimming dolphins. I pedal harder and faster. Lights are popping out all over now.

Beams of radiant colors burst through in pockets. Colors shoot in all directions like a laser light show.

"Tanz, can you hear me? Are you there?"

Still no response.

I pedal faster zooming around the Earth, amazed by this spectacle.

"Tanz, can you hear me? The most amazing thing is happening. The dark forces haven't won. We are," I say, almost skipping around the Earth. Reds, oranges, deep greens, and blues blast out of the toxic cloud.

I realize how excited I am seeing this heavenly light. As if everything good in me is coming alive.

"Tanz? Tanz?"

"Darkness cannot extinguish even the smallest light," he says.

I nod, zooming faster encircling, the globe. Light is penetrating the darkness... evaporating it... The cloud is thinning as the light expands.

I see the silhouettes again of spirits in these bright colors who simply smile and absorb their furious attacks and frightening howls with gentle love and acceptance. The attacks subside as the light increases.

The remaining dark forces pass through the light of spirts. Some turn to ash and cosmic debris. This reverse cleansing goes on for several more minutes.

Prisonface and Firearm try to escape back up into the portal. I get in their way ready to do some damage myself.

Firearm swings at me. I kick him back into an approaching light being. The spirit envelopes him. His face turns from anguish to serene as he turns to dust and floats off with the others.

Prisonface slips past into the portal that closes and evaporates into space. I look up and the portal black hole is gone. Stars shine in its place.

As the last of the dark forces are neutralized, the heavenly bodies above seem to sparkle a little brighter.

Slowly the spirits disband, swirling around me with brilliant lights and colors as if from a thousand pure mothers and fathers filled with universal love.

The smell of lilac and fresh flowers, wet earth, maple syrup and honey, fills my mind. Comforting sensations and smells—all the joys of life surround and fill me.

They float back to Earth's surface to complete their daily tasks all over the world and in every country. Even the most troubled regions…

I descend gradually allowing gravity to take over. Heat and steam come off my body. I drop slower beneath the cloud cover.

Rain begins falling across the entire world, even in places it hasn't rained in years. Spinning my legs over the continents less and less on my descending orbit, feeling a sense of rebirth. The rain cools me like a baptism. The heat subsides.

As fast as they came the raindrops stop. Yellow sunlight dazzles through the thinning clouds. I stop pedaling and surf down to Tanz in the financial district.

I'm smiling as if I just witnessed the birth of life itself.

"You did well…" He says as a proud father would nodding up at me.

"It was not me at all but the spirits." I'm giddy like a child landing on the sidewalk.

Tanz looks at my feet, "I will find you better shoes. Come. There is more work to be done." No rest for the weary or for the joyous.

He turns to walk. "This hidden battle is no longer hidden. Sides will be chosen. We must find Qualmsy and end his local reign."

"People just need a chance," I say.

Tanz nods. "Some will refuse. Yet the opportunity to evolve will be offered."

QUALMSY NETWORK

As we get downtown and watch his building for the right moment, it's around rush hour. A lot of people walk past while cars sit waiting to go. About to step out from behind the building we see Dino and Laurie-Ann shoved forward by his goons toward his warehouse.

"So innocent… You two are coming to work for us. Gonna make us a lot of money."

They shout *"No!"* and struggle to get free.

"Tanz, we have to help them."

"Then go. You are strong enough."

I nod. My legs begin pumping like a running back. I step out from the shadows and see the strangest thing.

Dino is growing larger. His face grows angry while his entire body glows blue like an electric fence. The men holding him get zapped and blown twenty feet in the air, crashing down onto cars, setting off their alarms half a block away. People look then quickly turn away, not wanting to get involved.

Dino and Laurie-Ann start to run.

"Dino, Laurie-Ann, wait up," I say. We catch up to them down the block.

Dino is normal again, though hyperventilating. "Reuben," he shouts from his sweet self, calming. "Who's that?" Dino points to Tanz standing behind me catching this breath.

Dino walks closer, poking him in the belly while looking up. This shocks Tanz with an electrical wave from Dino's fingertips. Tanz's blue eyes shimmer as he squats.

"Come closer, boy."

Tanz places his hands on Dino's chest and stomach and is instantly knocked to the ground.

"Cannot be…" he says, lying on the sidewalk. Blue imagery shimmers above him: a baby shooting into space from his wife onto a sunbeam and transported while a dark blade takes her life.

They look at him with mouths and eyes wide open. He leans up, muttering in disbelief. "My wife died. Our boy died." He pauses, then says to me, "Our boy died." I place my hand on his shoulder. He looks at me with tears, speaking ever so quietly. "My boy died." He then stares at Dino again.

His face is overcome with emotion, shock to tenderness, to joy and sorrow wrapped together. Tanz dives in, wrapping his arms around Dino while tears fall from his face. Dino lays his head on Tanz's shoulder. Laurie-Ann and I look at each other.

Tanz wipes away the image so as not to scare them. Leaning on one knee he releases him and asks, "Are you his mother?"

"No, I'm his sister. Our mom died when an electrical line fell and killed her as they walked."

I look at Tanz, that sounds familiar. She nods to Dino, patting his head, ruffling his hair. Tanz and I glance at each other.

"And what about your father?" he asks.

She shrugs. "He has a different father. But we never knew him. My mother was kind of a free spirit."

Tanz asks, "Has he grown big like that before, electric?"

Dino watches the adults converse.

"Only a few times, mostly when he doesn't get his way. Right, Dino?"

He playfully scowls up at her, crossing his arms.

"And can you do that?" Tanz asks her.

"No, not that."

He nods absently, clearly overwhelmed. I stand silently, my mind spinning, trying to understand.

Tanz says with a kindness in his voice I'd never heard before. "Since our families are gone, too, perhaps the four of us could be a family and watch out for one another?"

Laurie-Ann shrugs then glances at me. "Sure."

"Yay!" Dino hugs us both. I can see Tanz wanting to tell them more but not knowing how.

At Dino's level he says, "We have more work to do but we'll be back soon, okay? We'll play in the park. That's a promise. You guys go home now and stay safe."

He glances at them several times as they walk up the block. Creating a little equation in his hand, he holds it over his chest when it jumps into his heart.

*

We enter Qualmsy's building. There are no guards protecting it and no dark forces enveloping it. It's not cold and clammy. We get close to the main room and overhear, "No more, Mr. Qualmsy, I don't want to do this anymore... I want to see my mother." The woman who had come into the grocery store speaks to him on his red velvet couch.

Tattoo guy, standing near, says, "Come on, Doreen, let's go get a coffee. I'll take you to your mother's."

"You mean it, Sam?"

"Yeah, I mean it."

I lean over to Tanz. "There's nothing for us to do here."

He agrees and we walk out.

On the street, people walk in sunlight as remaining haze balls dissolve. The sunlight shines brighter than usual with a yellow the color of sunflowers. People are being released from imprisonment, turning away from the darkness.

One haze ball floats down the street as a sunbeam catches it. Legs pop out of the haze, then the body of a man. He takes one step then falls to his knees on the sidewalk weeping.

*

Near the waterfront we find the spirit lady tending to flowers on Business Street. The flowers grow as she tends to them. I look down the road and see half a dozen other spirits doing the same. They all glow with smiling colors, auras, energy fields surrounding them. The spirit lady looks up and smiles at us.

She approaches then encircles us with her colors. We're transported to another dimension.

"Where are we?" I ask Tanz through my forehead, looking around. My mouth is not working again. There's a bright light, azure clouds, and a sense of floating in a swimming pool on a warm day.

"We are here to visit God," Tanz says.

"What did you say?"

He doesn't answer, straightening his back. I know the Sun Clan works for the Gods but I, I have not. I swallow hard, looking around this strange place. Mostly just colors and odd shapes.

Every cell in my body is tingling, dancing, buzzing like static electricity.

Tanz nudges me. We kneel humbly in thanks.

His forehead pulsates with light. *"We are in your debt…"* Tanz says, bowing his head slapping me again. I am so stupefied I feel like if I say anything I would simply end up drooling on myself.

He/She/All chuckles in a pitch and sound that surrounds us from all directions. *"The Sun Clan owes no debt. There is only light and the choosing of light…"*

Tanz projects an inquiry: *"We must get to Narican yet cannot jump there. We must evolve, yet that will take too long. Can you help us?"*

"Ride the dimension energy wave. Find the entrance. It is a stream through all dimensions," He/She/All says, and is gone. *"Owes no debt at all."* we hear echoing.

*

Back in Big City, I fall to the ground needing to catch my breath as my body is overloaded. Too much happening. Nauseous and hot. I'm overwhelmed and need a moment.

Tanz says, "Before our journey, we must first stop for supplies."

"I must first stop right here. Just give me a moment, okay? I'm fighting dark forces, have spirit friends, and now I meet God?" I stumble over to a building stoop to sit down.

"Your first God?"

"Yes, Tanz, my first God."

"Then do take a moment. We will need crystals for our journey. It's only a few blocks from here. Then on to the energy wave."

I sit accepting that this is my new life. The cells in my body calm. I take a few more breaths then stand. "Yes, Tanz, my first God," I say rolling my eyes at him.

It's a warm day walking uptown when a question comes to me.

"When you went into the room at the hangar, you spoke to someone. Do you mind if I ask who?"

"That is my guide, an ancestor who is always with me."

I nod as we step off the curb at 38th to cross the street then back up onto the following sidewalk.

"Hmm." I get quiet for a moment as we continue. But then say, "A woman visits me. She comes through my thoughts with warnings and kindness. Who do you think she is?"

"She will reveal herself in time. Truth yearns to be known."

"Well, should I trust her?"

"She is part of you. Has she provided helpful knowledge in your best interest?"

I nod.

"Then yes, you must trust her as you would trust the very best of yourself."

Deep in thought we walk another few blocks.

"I still cannot believe he's my boy," Tanz says and stops walking. "Oh good, we're here."

I look up and see we're standing in front of Other Worlds.

He pulls open the door. Nan Nan stands behind the counter. She's a heavyset older woman with sparkling hazel eyes and wrinkled hands. Caser stands beside her and looks up.

"Mr. T," she says with her heavy accent.

"Good afternoon, Ms. M."

Ms. M, Nan Nan, stares at us. "Oh, I should have known you two were associated." She says jokingly.

Caesar and I slap hands and hug.

"Here are evolved ones, Claremone," Tanz says to me.

"Claremone?" Caesar says. "Dream Claremone? No *wayyy*."

I nod.

"Well, all right. Nan Nan, I told you he wasn't crazy."

She raises an eyebrow, laughs, and shoves him gently.

She reaches under the counter and pulls out a pouch, handing it to Tanz. "I believe you ordered these, Mr. T?"

"Thank you, Ms. M." He tucks them inside his shirt and pays her. "There is an associate I would like you to contact. One Mr. Milleron. He is part of a network you might be interested in joining. We must move on now yet will visit upon our return. Please call him at this number. And thank you again for your services."

As we step to the door, I look back at them. They feel like a family I'd lost and re-found.

Outside on the sidewalk Tanz says, "Now, let us get to the warship and energy wave."

"I didn't know you knew them," I say.

"I didn't know you did either. Like attracts like," he says.

Into no man's land we walk, firing up the ship. Tanz calculates the energy wave's time and location as it passes through this dimension. We take off above the city and zoom toward the Amazon jungle where it will soon return.

*

Deep in the forest, the jungle surrounds us. We track his calculations to a cliff of mud and roots. Jungle sounds fill the air.

He says, "Timing of the wave is imperative. I've calculated hopping on is equivalent to hopping on an express train at full speed with the doors closed."

"Great," I say, and almost slip down the muddy hillside trying to secure my feet in preparation. We stand at the edge of the muddy cliff waiting.

"We have .03 of a second to make the jump accurately...Never jump on the front of a wave. The middle is best."

The rippling waves of yellow energy come in like a fast-moving anaconda.

"No, not yet... Hold... Hold..." We wait for the peak of the right wave. Hitting off the side of a wave will knock us into space.

But the waves are moving too fast. They're blurring. I can't separate one from another.

"Hold... Hold..." Tanz says, calculating.

"I can't see it well enough. They're moving too fast," I say panicked.

"And... jump!"

We spring off the muddy earth. I grab a glowing ridge peak with my fingertips. The tremendous wind ripples my cheeks and clothes as it continues moving through the jungle, then exiting at the speed of light.

It leaves Earth heading into space.

"Hold on! Hold on!" Tanz shouts, having landed safely in the trough of a wave and reaching for me. Missing the peak and protection from the wind in the trough, my fingertips are slipping as we leave the third dimension.

THE END

Rise of The Narican King, is coming soon.

D.M. Robbins lives with his family in the
Catskill Mountains of New York.

Follow his work at www.dmrobbinsauthor.com.

Made in the USA
San Bernardino, CA
14 September 2019